HITCHED TO THE ALIEN GENERAL

WARRIORS OF THE LATHAR

MINA CARTER

NEW YORK TIMES & USA TODAY BESTSELLING AUTHOR

CONTENTS

*F*acing down the most dangerous warrior in the known universe was a bad idea. Facing down the most dangerous warrior in the known universe with a bad arm was suicide. But no one could ever accuse Xaandril, general of the Latharian forces, of being a coward. He centered himself, keeping his breathing as balanced as he was on the balls of his feet and studied the male in the circle with him.

Warriors crowded around the paint lines on the floor eagerly, jostling for the best place to view the fight. It wasn't often these two legendary warriors stepped in the circle during everyday training. Even the walkways overhead were crowded, the hum of whispered conversation a buzz in the air like a swarm of *gicandatias*.

All to see Xaan get his ass handed to him on a plate.

Because the male looking at him through narrowed eyes wasn't just *any* warrior. No. That would be too easy.

Daaynal K'Saan was the warrior emperor of the Lathar—a male who'd killed his first assassin when he was just a child and hadn't stopped fighting since. Like all Lathar, he was a warrior born and bred, honor braids thick through his hair. There was more braid than hair, each of them a battle honor.

Not that Xaan was counting. He knew how many honors Daaynal had. He knew the blood, sweat, and fury that had gone into gaining them because he'd stood beside him on the battlefield for each and every one, plus more than he could count besides.

And this fight was going to be a close one.

Xaan's eyes narrowed as the two paced around each other, like *deearin* alphas, the feline males sizing each other up before a battle to the death. He was a big male but Daaynal was easily as large as he was, and as heavily muscled. They both trained daily and had decades of experience on the battlefield and in the fight circles.

Because they weren't just ordinary warriors... they were emperor and champion. One had sworn an oath to the empire. The other had sworn to protect him. Right now though, that oath was going to do Xaan *draanth* all good.

He moved opposite to Daaynal, watching for the first move. He knew from long experience not to let himself get distracted. Daaynal would kick his ass to the Teranis sector and back.

Instead of waiting for Daaynal to make the first move, Xaan roared and charged. He was rewarded with a small look of surprise in his opponent's eyes as he wrapped Daaynal up in a wrestling move he'd recently learned and dumped him on his ass right there in the middle of the circle.

A shocked gasp went up from the warriors assembled as the two went down in a tangle of limbs to the hard floor. Xaan's shoulder ended up in Daaynal's stomach as they hit, all the air exiting the emperor's lungs in a solid *ummmph.*

Xaan flipped easily on the floor, twisting with limber grace unusual in such a big man. He managed to keep Daaynal pinned, his good arm around the emperor's neck as he stretched the other male out with a knee in the small of his back, Daaynal's spine in a hard curve.

He grinned, triumph running through his veins as he tried to flick Daaynal's hair out of his face and hold on at the same time. It didn't work. The emperor's long, dark hair obscured his vision, but he didn't need to see to hold on to his quarry.

Watching old holovids from the newly discovered Earth had had an unexpected side effect. He'd discovered several new fighting styles to add to his repertoire. Who would have thought that humans, the descendants of a lost Lathar expedition, would have developed so many different and effective methods of combat?

Daaynal wasn't a warrior emperor for nothing though. With a heave and a flip, he dislodged the hold and managed to get an arm free to slam into Xaan's ribcage, just under his healing arm. Agony flared through his torso, transmitted by his ribcage, and greedy tendrils of pain caressed every nerve ending he had. Sucking in a hard breath, he held on like grim death with his good arm.

Daaynal struck again, the edge of the blow catching Xaan's bad arm. This time the pain was agony. A burst white-hot enough to rival even the most intense star centered in his shoulder. For a moment it felt like all the damage that had been healed months ago was raw and new, like his shoulder was nothing more than a mass of broken bones and raw, pulped flesh.

Despite the pain he held on grimly—for all of a few seconds. Through it all, he remembered this wasn't a fight to the death. He wasn't on a battlefield. Not anymore. Instead, he was in a fight circle with the male who had been his lifelong friend, and this was a training match, nothing more.

Even so, he was in a circle with the emperor—a warrior who had never been beaten... who *could* never be beaten. If Xaan beat him, even in training, Daaynal's competence as a warrior would be called into question. That would invite challenges for the throne... which, to borrow a phrase from the humans who had become a fixture at court... was a whole level of shit they didn't need. Not with the uncertain situation with humanity at present and the purists who wanted the newly discovered race wiped out of existence.

But, all that being said, there was no way he was going to make it easy for Daaynal. He wouldn't want that. He ruled because he *was* a warrior emperor, not because he played at it.

With a groan of pain that was not feigned, Xaan felt his grip slip a little. Seeing an opening, Daaynal slammed an elbow up again, catching Xaan in the side. Pain blossomed once more, but it was an easier agony to ride out this time, nothing like having his shoulder pounded on.

He was forced to let go as Daaynal twisted, and then he found the tables reversed as the big emperor, ever the quick learner, tried to pin him with a similar move. But he wasn't going to get caught like that. The press of warriors crowded around the circle snapped back into his awareness as they gasped. He ignored them in favor of throwing himself to the side, breaking Daaynal's grip and rolling away.

Beating the emperor in a circle fight would be a bad thing, but he also had enough male pride to not want to be beaten himself. Especially not with a certain delicate human female in the crowds watching the fight.

Kenna Reynolds, one of the females—women, he corrected himself. They preferred to be called women, not females—they'd taken from the first human base they'd found, stood there, balanced on the edge of the paint line as though ready to throw herself in the circle. Whether to protect him or to protect Daaynal *from* him, Xaan wasn't sure.

His entire body tensed, ready in case she did something stupid and tried to get between them. Ice rolled down his spine at the thought. She was a warrior of her own people, a marine she called herself, and he'd seen her fight, but she was tiny compared to them. She could be so easily hurt. Worse...

The flick of Daaynal's gaze toward the human told Xaan he'd been caught, and a smile spread over the big male's face. With a sigh, he swept his hair back off his face and rolled his shoulders until one clicked. Stepping back, he gave a small bow. The respect of one warrior to another.

"An excellent bout, as always, Champion," he rumbled in the deep rasp he was known for. "But I have other matters to attend to, so we will have to adjourn for today. Tomorrow I'll kick your ass good and proper though."

Xaan's face split into a broad grin. "You and whose army, *Your Majesty?*"

"I don't need an army to deal with you, champion or no champion."

Their good-natured banter continued as they stepped out of the circle and grabbed the towels they'd left on the bench by the wall. The crowd that had been watching them broke up and returned to their own circles, bouts filling the main training hall.

Kenna went with a group, he noted, casting a

quick glance back over her shoulder toward Xaan and Daaynal. The warriors she was with were younger ones, all eager to learn human moves that would give them an edge against bigger, stronger warriors. It was a technique started on the *Veral'vias* and was gaining popularity.

He thought he'd kept his interest to himself, grabbing a towel to wipe his neck down, but he'd learned one thing from being the emperor's champion for all these years. And that was Daaynal didn't miss *a thing.*

"When are you going to get off your ass and claim that woman?" the big emperor commented in a low voice, eyes bright as he took a long swallow from his water bottle. His pale gaze cut across the hall to where Kenna was training, a lithe figure moving gracefully between the younger warriors.

Longing and desire rose up, sharp and immediate, as soon as he looked at her. Ruthlessly, he schooled his expression in case they were being watched—the emperor and champion were *always* being watched in some way or other—but he couldn't stop the lingering look at the human female.

He shrugged in reply to Daaynal's question. He wanted to claim her. More than wanted to. The idea of having her as his mate, of pulling her delicate slenderness against him and claiming her lips for the first time, haunted him at night. Every moment he was around her made it harder and harder to resist the temptation to growl the words and tie them together for life.

"How can I?" he asked, lifting his damaged arm.

It moved, but not as easily as before. He'd been lucky. The best healer in the empire, Laarn—Daaynal's sister son and the empire's lord healer—had been on hand when he'd been injured in battle. Without his work, Xaan knew he wouldn't be worrying about a dodgy arm. He wouldn't be worrying about anything. His wounds had been so extensive he should have been dead on the battlefield.

But still, a warrior without two good arms was worthless. He was only half the male he should be.

Daaynal's gaze flicked down to Xaan's arm, no longer in a sling, and he shrugged. "So? You'll get full mobility back... What other male could manage to last so long against me? Even with two good arms."

He had a point. Xaan rumbled in the middle of his chest as he took the water bottle Daaynal held out to him.

"I'm too old for her," he argued, only to be given a withering look by his friend. "She should pick someone younger."

"Trallshit." Daaynal was having none of his excuses. "You're a male in your prime. And does it look like she wants a younger warrior?"

He nodded toward the group Kenna was with. Even from this distance it was easy to see that her opponent in the ring was doing his best to be charming. She dumped him on his ass without batting an eyelid and motioned to one of the others to take his place. The dismissed warrior slunk away to the back of the group, shame-faced.

"That doesn't mean anything."

It didn't. Training in the circles was completely different from saddling herself with a male who was only half a warrior for the rest of her life. He kept his thoughts to himself as he drank. Daaynal meant well, but how could he compete with warriors like... well Daaynal himself, and his sister sons. Hells, even Xaan's own son had found a human female of his own. But they were more progressive, less rooted in the past.

"Sure... sure, you keep telling yourself that," Daaynal snorted, grabbing his wrist as Xaan handed back the water bottle. His gaze cut down to the tatty blue ribbon tied around Xaan's wrist and back up. Xaan's cheeks heated. Kenna had tied it around his wrist at the court tournament months ago.

"Perhaps you might want to take the lady's favor off then if you're not interested in her. Give others a shot."

"Fuck off. It's just a ribbon." Xaan yanked his hand back. He'd told himself that many times. That it was just a ribbon. It didn't mean anything. Yet he couldn't bring himself to take it off.

"Yeah... yeah, you keep telling yourself that, lover-boy," Daaynal winked and threw his towel over one broad shoulder. "Claim her before someone else does. Don't make me make it an order."

SHE COULD DO this court thing. Wear a dress, check. Feel like a princess, check. No one needed to know she had her combat boots on under the swishy full-length skirt or that she had a dagger strapped to her thigh. As her friend Jane was fond of saying... you could take the girl out the marines, but you could never take the marine out the girl.

Kenna hid her smile and paused in the doorway to the hall. The scent of cologne and leather hit her like a wave with the low hum of voices following closely behind. With several war groups holding positions around the emperor's flagship, the *Miisan-vuis*, the large hall was packed with Latharian warriors in their leathers and colored sashes. The occasional female here and there wore silken dresses much like the one Kenna wore.

A few she vaguely recognized from Sentinel Five, the base she'd been stationed at before the Lathar had discovered humanity, but some were new. Idly she wondered how they'd ended up here, but then she spotted a familiar, determined face in the crowd and grinned.

Jane, formerly Major Allen of the Terran Marine Corps, now Lady Jane K'Vass, approached with her mate Karryl a step or two behind. Like Kenna, she was dressed in a Latharian-style gown, but silver instead of scarlet.

"Fucking *hell*, they've crammed them in tonight. Haven't they?" Jane said, folding Kenna into a quick hug before casting a glance down her in assessment. "You look good, girl. That color suits you."

"Thanks," Kenna couldn't help a little twirl to show off. Jane's lips quirked and she reached out to Kenna's skirts, lifting them a touch to reveal the boots beneath.

Kenna shrugged. "In case we need to kick ass and take names. Remember Cat's wedding?"

"Oh yes. Good times, eh?" Jane chuckled, a wide grin on her face. Cat had been the first human woman married to a Latharian warrior, and their wedding had been gatecrashed by purists unhappy about the union. It had turned into an all-out gun battle until the bride had shot a purist point-blank and proved to all the Lathar that human women weren't to be trifled with.

Jane parted her own skirts to give a quick glimpse of her thigh. Kenna grinned. Like her, Jane was wearing combat boots and she had a small handgun in a thigh holster.

Karryl sighed, shaking his head in fond amusement. "She never goes anywhere without it." It was easy to tell from the affection in his voice it was something he didn't discourage. In fact, his tone was proud.

"Hey, hey, look at you with the short hair. I heard about the promotion. Congratulations!"

Kenna included him in her good mood, smiling up at the tall warrior. Like the rest, he was dressed in leathers with a wide sash across his chest. But the long hair he'd had the last time she'd seen him was gone, replaced with a short back and sides to indicate his new rank of war commander.

"Thank you, Lady Kenna. You are most kind." He inclined his head in reply, but the grin soon returned. When she'd first met him, he'd been rather dour and grumpy, but obviously married life agreed with him.

"Fuck *me,*" Jane breathed, the glass in her hand paused halfway to her lips in shock. "Is that General Black over there?"

Kenna followed her gaze across the ballroom to a small, dark-haired woman on the arm of a broad-shouldered light-haired warrior. Instantly she recognized them.

"It is... was." She snagged herself a glass off the tray of a circling waiter, a younger warrior pressed into service for the evening. "She's Dani K'Vass now. That's Sardaan, her mate. He's the comms officer on the *Veral'vias.*"

Jane nodded, sipping at her drink. It was just fruit juice. As much as human women had proved they were a match for their Latharian mates, some of the alcoholic beverages the Lathar drank could make them seriously ill.

"I heard there was some bullshit going on back home?"

"Some?" Kenna sighed. Screw the fruit juice. She needed something stronger for this particular conversation.

"It's totally FUBAR down there. Vice President Cole was in talks with Fenriis and the bigwigs before the emperor arrived, which was going well... only then Halland had a brain fart and got in bed with Radcliffe and Hopkins. Hopkins decided it would be a good idea to try and take over the *Veral'vias*... Yeah, I know. Dumb huh?" she said as Jane blinked in surprise.

"That's when Black had to wade in to try and sort it out. She managed to get Cole back but then Radcliffe joined in drinking the loopy-juice and attacked the ship again to try and kidnap the emperor. This time they lost all three teams, BUT..." She held her hand up as Jane went to say something.

"More importantly, at the same time they managed to convict Cole of vote rigging and fraud. Sent her to Mirax Ruas, which I think is what *that* over there is about." She nodded toward where the emperor was surrounded by a small group of warriors from the *Veral'vias*. Danaar was speaking animatedly, his large body tense.

Jane whistled lowly. "What a fuckup. They do

realize humanity couldn't win against the Lathar. Right?"

"You'd think. Wouldn't you." Kenna replied absently, her attention hijacked as a new figure appeared in the small group around the emperor. As tall and heavily muscled as Daaynal himself, his short, dirty-blond hair stood out among a sea of darker, long-haired warriors.

Xaandril, the emperor's champion.

He scrubbed up well, his leathers clean and polished. Unlike a lot of the warriors in the room, he didn't wear a sash across his broad chest. They were worn to signify what role the warrior held aboard the ship he was stationed to. Xaandril didn't wear one because he wasn't assigned to any one ship. Warriors nearby gave the group a wide berth when he glared at them.

"Still hankering after tall, blond and growly?"

Jane jostled her lightly in the ribs and she realized Karryl had wandered off, talking with a pair of warriors a short distance away. She and her former boss were alone in the middle of the crowded room. A sigh escaped Kenna as she snuck another glance over at the handsome champion.

"Yeah. Still doesn't seem to notice the fact I'm

bloody female though," she groused lightly, trying not to let it get to her.

Xaandril blew hot and cold. One moment she was sure he liked her and was about to finally kiss her. The next he treated her the same as any of the younger warriors aboard. She never knew where she stood with him.

"Men," Jane snorted. "No matter the species, no telling what goes through their heads. Tell him and if he doesn't feel the same, walk away."

2

*K*enna was at the ball. In a dress.

Those two thoughts blocked everything else out of Xaan's mind, not allowing any others to form. He stood next to the emperor, aware that he should be listening to the conversation going on, but all he could do was nod dumbly as he snuck glances across the room.

She was utterly beautiful. The deep scarlet of her dress highlighted the perfection of her creamy skin, offset by the dark hair swept up into an arrangement of curls atop her head. He loved her hair, a deep, rich color full of browns and reds he'd never seen before.

The arch of her delicate neck as she leaned closer to the woman with her reminded him for a moment of his long dead mate, Laryssa. She'd been beautiful and delicate, and he'd thought himself madly in love with her. Perhaps he had been, but any pain of her passing was gone, and now she was just a memory from his past. What he felt for the human woman, a warrior like him, was sharp and immediate—stronger than anything he could ever remember feeling for Laryssa.

He hadn't acted on his feelings though. He'd been going to after the tournament when she'd given him the ribbon he still wore around his wrist, but he'd ended up in the battle that had nearly killed him. Recovery had been long and hard, and he'd been convinced that a woman like Kenna, a warrior in her own culture, would never want a male who was less than a man.

But Daaynal's words earlier weighed on his mind, and a sideways glance confirmed that yes, his friend had realized why Xaan wasn't participating in the conversation. Something about the acting commander of the *Veral'vias* wanting to head off to infiltrate a Terran prison facility to get back the former human vice president... he didn't know why she was there, nor why she'd been removed from her previous position because he wasn't following the conversation.

Instead, his attention was on the warrior

swaggering across the room. His destination was obvious. Kenna and her companion, Karryl K'Vass's mate, were the only two females in that area of the room. He sucked a breath in, irritation tensing all his muscles as he mentally urged the warrior, *move along draanthic. Nothing for you there.*

Lathar weren't telepathic though and the warrior continued to make a beeline for the two women. Kenna turned and looked up at him, her expression rapt as he said something. Then the brightest smile spread across her beautiful face and Xaan gritted his teeth to keep from punching something.

But it got worse. Kenna nodded and put her hand on the warrior's arm before he led her out onto the dance floor. Jealousy hit Xaan hard and fast, the growl starting in the center of his chest before he could stop it. Excusing himself from the emperor's presence with a small bow, he strode across the ballroom, intercepting them before they reached the dance floor.

"My dance, I believe," he growled, barely recognizing his own voice. His glare was all for the other male, ignoring Kenna for a moment, as he stepped closer and used his bigger frame to intimidate. It was a dick move, but he didn't care. He didn't want the other male... *any* other male touching her. Not as long as he drew breath.

"General," the other warrior sensibly decided retreat was the better part of valor and ceded the field, nodding to Kenna. "Perhaps another time, my lady."

Over my dead body. Xaan barely managed to restrain the urge to follow the male and throw him into a challenge circle, and he half-turned to see Kenna watching him with a curious expression. He didn't trust himself to speak so he simply held out a hand. She was his, but he wouldn't force her to do anything. If she wanted to be with him, she had to make the decision.

Reality narrowed down to just the two of them as her gaze flicked from his face down to his hand and back again. An emotion he couldn't name flittered in the backs of her eyes, gone before he could identify it, and she reached out. He sucked in a hard breath, a tingle going through his body at the first touch of her delicate fingers against his.

She was a warrior of her own people, fearsome and capable. Hells, the first time he'd seen her, she'd had the muzzle of a pistol pressed against a warrior's skull because he'd threatened her friend. But in that moment all his instincts told him she was delicate and female, his to protect.

Fingers closing around hers, he led her onto the dance floor. Silence charged with awareness swelled between them as he turned and pulled her close. She fit perfectly, her slender body nestled against his larger one as though she'd been made by the lady goddess to be there. To be his.

They shared a breath as his hand spread over her lower back, the touch far closer to a caress than any he'd given her before. They'd never danced, he realized. They'd trained together, yes, up to his injury... but he'd never held her in his arms like he was now. Chest to chest, his hand held her captive against him. His other hand held hers, her fingers so slender and delicate against his.

A shudder rolled down his spine at the way she rested trustingly against him. She was so strong, but he could snap her in two without breaking a sweat. It made him feel like the ravening beast he was, especially where she was concerned. Trying to keep his mind off how she'd feel pressed against him naked, he turned them into the first steps of the dance.

"Why did you do that?" she asked, curiosity on

her beautiful, heart-shaped face. "Run that warrior off. He only wanted to dance."

The answer was simple. "Dancing leads to thoughts of other things. So if you're dancing, you're dancing with me."

There, it was out. The feeling of possessiveness, that she was his and his alone, that he'd harbored close to his heart for so long.

Her face was unreadable. "So you've decided it then? What if I want to dance with someone else?"

"Then you'll be responsible for bloodshed. Do you want that?"

"What if I want to dance with Daaynal?" She arched an eyebrow and answered a question with a question, a quirk in her lips that said she thought she'd won the argument.

He didn't try to stop the growl as he pulled her closer, his hand spreading out over the back of her hips. "Why? You have an eye on being empress now? Because if it comes to you, that match only ends one way."

For her, he'd take on anyone... even his oldest friend.

Her eyes widened at the growled declaration, and her breath hitched in the most delightful way. Hiding a small smile, he swept her out of the ballroom on the next turn and into one of the darkened corridors that surrounded it.

"Too crowded in there," he murmured to her puzzled look. It was a blatant excuse. He just wanted her to himself for a while. Her little smile as his steps slowed said she saw right through him.

He slowed in the darkest part of the corridor until they were doing little more than swaying together to the soft music that filtered out from the ballroom.

"You look..."

Draanth. When had it gotten so difficult to talk to a female? He didn't remember courting being this nerve racking. It was like his brain had short-circuited and all he could do was look down at her in awe. Quite why she was out here with a scarred old warrior like him, he didn't know, but she wasn't fighting to get away, so he'd take it.

And whatever else she was willing to give him.

"I look what?" she asked, her voice a soft murmur as she looked up at him. His attention was hijacked by the soft brush of her fingers against his shoulder and for a moment he wished he wasn't in full uniform. He wanted to feel her touch against his skin there.

"Beautiful."

He managed to get his thoughts in order finally and was rewarded with a burst of pleasure in her dark eyes along with a soft smile. Normally she was hard-bitten and sassy, giving him cheek right on back when he growled, so the hint of a softer side to her got to him on levels he hadn't expected.

Her hand slid up to the side of his neck as she lifted on her toes, lips parted in invitation. His thought processes cut off, his body reacting on pure instinct as his free hand brushed her cheek and buried itself in her hair. He leaned down.

The sound of someone clearing their throat froze them both in place.

"Errr... General? The emperor requests your presence."

Xaan sighed, closing his eyes for a second.

Cock-blocked by the emperor himself.

Great. Just *draanthing* great.

"We'll be right there."

All Kenna's feminine instincts howled in frustration at the interruption. Xaan had nearly kissed her. So nearly kissed her that she'd almost felt the brush of his lips against hers. So nearly kissed her that she physically ached and had to bite back her moan when he pulled away.

Their gazes caught and held. Her heart skipped a beat at the heat in his eyes. Like all Lathar, his eyes were cat-like, but at the moment his pupils were dilated so much he almost looked human.

He hadn't let her go, the hard arm around her waist pulling her up against him. She knew he was fit, ripped even... but knowing that and seeing that was very different from being pressed up close and personal against him.

"We have to go," he murmured, his voice deeper than she'd ever heard it before. It did things to her on a primal level, ones that heated her blood and should be illegal. Leaning down, he surprised her by nuzzling his nose against hers in a soft, sexy little movement. "But hold that thought."

He let her go. She missed the heat of his body against hers instantly, and was forced to bite back a pout of disappointment. He smiled as though he could read her thoughts and slid his hand down her arm to capture her hand in his.

The unexpected possessive gesture silenced her as they followed the warrior through the corridors toward the war room. Unusually, it was mostly empty.

Only Daaynal sat at the large table, a frown on his face as he read from what looked like a thin sheet of plastic —a flex-pad probably linked to the ship's database.

He looked up as they entered the room and nodded to them. "General. Lady Kenna." His gaze flittered down to their linked hands but he didn't comment, just motioned to the table. "Please. Sit."

"What's this about?" Xaan asked as he pulled a seat out for Kenna and made sure she was settled before taking the one next to her. His tone was level but she caught the irritation and frustration hidden there. Mostly because she shared them. What could be so important that the emperor had called him out of a formal function?

"The bridge crew informed me of some strange readings," Daaynal said, pushing not one, but two pads over the table.

"What kind of readings?" Xaan asked, picking his pad up and studying it with interest. "Surely the bridge crew can handle this?"

Kenna picked up the one that came to a stop in front of her. It flickered on to show a star chart on one side and numbers on the other. It was in Latharian, the geometric writing not making much sense to her. A quick scan of the page revealed a small symbol in the top corner.

She suppressed a grin, recognizing the Latharian symbol for danger overlaid onto a female figure. Someone had a sense of humor. She agreed. Human women *were* dangerous. Far more than the Latharians had been prepared for.

Pressing the symbol, she waited for a second as the pad reconfigured itself to display in English. Then she frowned and looked up at Daaynal.

"This is one of the outer colony systems, Delta Orellius... It's a bit off the beaten track. Only the more extreme colonists head out that way."

She'd listened to her uncle rabbit on and on about the region after the woman he'd wanted to marry upped and joined an expedition to Delta Orellius years before she was born. To hear him tell it, the place was filled with extreme doomsday preppers and survivalist nutjobs.

Daaynal nodded, and she knew the information had been filed away. She liked that about the Latharian emperor. He could have been totally up himself and arrogant, yet he was anything but. He listened to everyone, from the most highly decorated general right down to the lowliest warrior, and nothing got past him, not even the smallest detail.

"We knew it was a Terran-held system, which is why the bridge crew flagged it. The readings are not typical for that kind of system, nor are they Terran in origin."

"Oh?" Kenna sat forward in interest. "What kind of readings are they then?"

"They're not sure." Xaan frowned, reading through the information on the data-pad. "The results don't match up with anything in our databases. Used to be a science officer," he added by way of explanation and then smiled at her look of surprise. "Before I realized war was my calling."

"Oh. Of course." Kenna sat back in surprise. She'd spent so long thinking of him as the war veteran general, hero of his people, that she'd never considered he'd been a warrior before he'd become Daaynal's champion. But he must have been. He must have served aboard a ship somewhere, and the last time she checked, "future general" wasn't a job opening.

"A man of many talents," she commented with a smile.

"Don't tell him that. He'll get a fat head and we won't get him through the door," Daaynal chuckled. "But he is quite right. The *aratak* and *evistron* levels are off the charts, which is unusual for a system with a *Treaniis* class star like this one. No evidence of faster-than-light engines, which could account for the levels, so it's not non-Terran ships."

She shook her head. "No, there wouldn't be... Delta Orellius is an old system, charted back in the early days of colonization. Back then they would have used sleeper ships. It takes months to get new blood and supplies out there even now."

"No unusual frequencies either?"

Xaan pursed his lips as Daaynal shook his head. "I had them rerun the scans twice. Same results."

The big champion grunted and sat back in his chair. "Send a ship to investigate. It's better to be safe than sorry."

Daaynal twirled his stylus between his fingers like a street magician with a coin. "Just what I thought. However, considering the current state of affairs with the Terrans, I don't wish to split the fleet."

Xaan shrugged. "Send a long-range scout. Doesn't need to be a warship to get eyes on."

Kenna looked from one to the other, sure there was a conversation going on she wasn't privy to.

"Exactly what I was thinking. You'll take the *Jerri'tial*. If you leave tonight you can be in system within... seventy-two hours."

"Wait... what? Me? I can't go."

Xaan glared across the table while Kenna hid her grin. It was easy to see the two were friends. No one else would dare speak to the warrior emperor that way.

"Of course you can. You are." Daaynal's voice was firm, an edge of amusement in his eyes as he slid a glance at Kenna. "Take the good lady here. It's Terran space, so by all rights you should have a representative with you."

"He does have a point." Kenna turned to Xaan. "I was born on a colony very similar to the ones in the system. I know how they work. How their systems work... in case we have a problem. Not that we'll have any problems," she added quickly.

"See?" Daaynal grinned and flicked his hair from his face as he leaned back in his chair. "Perfect solution. Take the *Jerri'tial, and* report back what you find."

3

_T_raveling in a space ship on a super-secret mission had sounded so exciting. In reality, it sucked. Big donkey balls sucked. With a sigh, Kenna leaned her head back against the seat and watched Xaan at the pilot's console.

"If you're tired," he said without taking his eyes from the screen in front of him, "you should go and get some sleep. We still have a long journey ahead of us."

"I'm not tired," she said quickly, turning to the side and bringing her knees up to curl up in the copilot's seat.

She could watch him forever. For such a big man, his movements were filled with an economic grace that she found fascinating. He'd stopped wearing the arm-sling a while back, but she knew the bad shoulder still bothered him. Not that he'd ever mention any discomfort, especially to her. He was the least talkative guy she knew, of any species. But over the months she'd been with the Lathar, she'd learned to read his moods. In a way.

"Besides," she added with a look back into the main cabin of the ship. "It's empty."

She'd always traveled in larger Latharian vessels before. Warships were huge, designed to carry small armies of warriors, and built on lines that made her feel like a child. So, stepping into the small confines of the scout ship had been a change. The sense of strangeness was reinforced by the fact the inside was completely bare. Where she'd have expected to see interior fittings—crew seats, bunks, etc.—there was nothing but bare metal walls.

Xaan slid her a sideways glance and smiled with little more than a quirk of his lips at the corners.

"It's magic." He winked and pressed a button on the console.

She gasped as the back portion of the cabin came to life. Sections of paneling depressed and moved out of the way as furniture unfolded from the walls and assembled itself. Within seconds what had been a bare room became a fully appointed bedroom.

With one bed.

She arched an eyebrow at him. "You think you're getting lucky, handsome?"

His smile broadened. "Oh, I'm already lucky. I've got the most beautiful female in the galaxy to myself for the next few days."

She blinked, her surprise showing on her face. For months, they'd been wrapped up in a delicate dance around each other. She'd seen him at his lowest, near death's door, and he'd helped her navigate an alien society that was nothing like her own. Half the time she'd been convinced he was about to make a claim on her, seeing the male interest in his eyes, but until the dance he'd never once said anything or flirted with her.

Until now. This was flirting. Wasn't it?

Her eyes narrowed. "Okay. Who are you? And what did you do with my friend Xaan?"

He laughed, the deep, rich sound filling the interior of the small ship. The sound didn't get to her as much as the expression on his face. The little lines at the corners of his eyes crinkled up. Even the big scar across his face, the one she'd found so scary at first, twisted up by his lips.

"I compliment you and your first thought is I'm a *kinatash?*"

"A what, where?" she asked, sidetracked for a moment. Even though she'd had the standard neuro-translator implanted months ago, some Latharian words had no direct translation.

"Ermmm..." He thought for a moment. "A face liar? Someone who uses another being's appearance?"

Realization hit. "Oh, like a shape shifter?" She was instantly all ears. It would make so much sense if there were such beings. "Changes form?"

"Yes, exactly. You have such things on Terra?"

Kenna shook her head. "No, not really. They're just stories. Myths and legends."

"All stories have a basis in fact somewhere," he said as he turned to tap out a series of commands on the console in front of him. The low voice of the computer announced, "autopilot engaged," and he levered himself up to walk into the back of the cabin. "The *kinatash* are rare now, but every so often we come across one."

"Oh? Why are they rare?"

She followed him, almost walking right into his back when he stopped abruptly. Instantly she knew she'd hit on something, his broad shoulders tense as he ran a hand through his hair.

"The *Ovverta*," he said quietly.

She froze, the name alone sending chills down her spine. She didn't know much about Xaan's early life but she'd been able to piece together some of it. His family had been killed by a species called *Ovverta*, and he'd hunted them down to extinction in revenge. She didn't know much about them though. She'd asked but they were like the Lathar's version of the bogeyman. No one wanted to talk about them.

Moving carefully, she laid her hand in the center of his back. "It's okay. You don't have to tell me anything else."

"The cabin reconfigures itself on command," he said, as though she hadn't said anything. She lifted her hand, giving him room. He'd talk when he was ready. She'd learned long ago that Xaan was a man of few words at times.

"Facilities are in the back, left door. Right door is to the cargo space. Don't go in there," he warned. "It's got less insulation than the cabin so it gets cold."

"Yes, sir." She snapped off a quick salute, falling back into her usual cheery, slightly teasing act. She grabbed her pack from where she'd dropped it behind the copilot's seat. "Dibs on the shower first."

. . .

GRABBING her wash kit and towel, she disappeared into the bathroom. After a few seconds being amazed that they could fit everything, including a fully functioning shower, into the tiny space, she stripped down and stepped into the shower.

Conscious of the hot water, and that Xaan had to shower after her, she showered as quickly as she could. It didn't take her long after that to emerge dressed in the shorts and tank top she usually slept in.

"All yours," she said with a smile, trying not to notice he was sitting on the side of the bed closest to her, stripped to the waist. One thing was for sure... like most Latharian warriors, he was *very* nicely built. Unlike most though, his arms from his elbows up to his shoulders were covered in crisscross, oddly colored tattoos. But they weren't really tattoos. They were scars. He'd burned them into his own skin with the acidic blood of some kind of alien snake.

She shivered at the very idea. Tattoos were bad enough, needles driving ink into the skin, but she couldn't imagine the pain as acid etched the design instead.

"Thanks," he hauled himself up and headed into

the bathroom. A second later she heard the water snap on again. Hopefully she'd left him enough hot water. Used to water rationing from the corps, she was used to showering quickly so she should have.

Draping her still damp towel over the back of the copilot's chair to dry, she headed back to the bed. It was large, designed for Latharians, so easily larger than a queen size. Biting her lip, she debated which side to take.

It was just a barracks situation, she told herself. Despite the almost kiss at the ball earlier and his "hold that thought," he hadn't said anything else or tried to kiss her again.

Which was Xaandril all over.

Trying not to let frustration get the better of her, she picked the side of the bed nearest to her and slid under the covers. Her toes curled as her warm skin met the cool sheets. She curled up into a little ball until the bed warmed up.

Wriggling, she got comfortable, being careful not to encroach on Xaan's side of the bed. Just a barracks situation, she told herself again. Hopefully this time it would sink in. Instead of the bunks being one above the other, they were just side by side without a dividing wall.

She sighed as she snuggled down. Like most

Latharian beds, it was like sleeping in a cloud that hugged her entire body. The blanket was lightweight and silky, but as cozy as any Terran sleeping bag or duvet. One thing was for sure... she *never* wanted to sleep in a Terran bed again.

A sound from the bathroom made her open her eyes and she realized that Xaan hadn't latched the door properly. At some point during his shower it had swung open a little, giving her a clear view of Xaan's back as he stood at the sink, cleaning his teeth. Her eyes widened as her gaze traveled down and she realized he wasn't wearing a towel. The firm, taut globes of his naked ass were in full view.

Holy hell, she bit back a very feminine whimper. He was just as drool-worthy without his clothes on.

Instantly, though, she shut her eyes. He didn't realize she was watching him, and she wouldn't want to be spied on without her knowledge. So it wasn't fair to assume it was okay just because he was a guy.

I wouldn't mind him spying... a little voice in the back of her mind whispered, but she ignored it for the moment and turned over. Less temptation that way.

Relaxing her body, she concentrated on falling asleep. She let her muscles go lax as she cleared her mind, imagining herself in a hammock under a starlit sky. It was a trick all marines were taught to fall asleep quickly, even in a foxhole in the middle of a battlefield. The hammock might change for whatever the individual preferred to visualize, but the concept was the same.

It had the right effect. Within a minute she felt her muscles relax and her body settle further into the embrace of the bed. She breathed out, a soft sigh of contentment only disturbed when the mattress shifted as Xaandril climbed into bed.

She expected him to settle down on his side and turn his back to fall asleep like she was. They had no idea what they'd be facing when they reached their destination, so being well-rested would give them the best advantage. Tired people made crap decisions.

She certainly didn't expect a strong arm to snake around her waist, or to be pulled into the protective lea of his bigger body. He chuckled, his deep voice soft in her ear as she started a little. "I had no idea humans could fall asleep so quickly."

"Practice," she mumbled, wriggling to cuddle against him. No way was she going to pass up the opportunity. So he wasn't a talker... if he was a cuddler they could work it out. They could work anything out if they both wanted it enough, even the differences between Lathar and human.

"You're cute." His lips grazed her temple. "And so delicate it scares me."

She was careful to keep her body relaxed and her eyes closed. If he was only talking because he thought she was half asleep, she didn't want to wake fully and scare him off. Stop him talking.

"Not delicate," she told him, yawning and pillowing her head on his strong arm. "Marine, remember?"

It felt nice being held by him, and the gentle touch of his big hand on her hip wasn't inappropriate. Not that she would have been bothered if it was. She'd long ago decided that, of all the handsome Latharian warriors, Xaandril was the only one she would accept. The only one she could see herself spending a lifetime with.

"Yeah, but you're human. I could break you in two without breaking a sweat."

"Creepy much?" She snorted.

He stiffened. "I would never hurt you."

She patted his arm, her lips quirking a little in amusement. "I know. I was only teasing."

He rumbled under his breath, the sound transferring through his broad chest pressed against her back. Silence fell for long moments, but then, just as she thought he'd started to fall asleep, he spoke again.

"Laryssa was delicate as well. Taller than you are, and so beautiful," he started slowly, his voice low and almost absent... as though he didn't realize he was speaking aloud. A stab of jealousy surged through her for a moment but instantly she beat it down. Laryssa had been his mate's name. The one who had died.

"But delicate. Too delicate. She struggled to cope even with the protected lifestyle I could give her. Bearing our daughter was almost too much for her, and sometimes..." He shrugged, his hold on her moving slightly.

"I don't know... I felt more like a guardian than her mate. Like she was too good and delicate for me. But then the *Ovverta* attacked our home planet. We'd settled on one of the outer ring planets, a lovely place with the lilac seas she loved," he added. "I was away, in service. Back then I was a commander with a war group of my own."

She stroked the inside of his arm gently. She'd wondered why he had short hair when most warriors wore their hair long with braided battle honors. The only Lathar with short hair were the commanders, like the generals of the Latharian army, who'd risen so high they'd gone past the need to count personal honors and instead put their efforts to the glory of the empire.

"When I got back, they were all dead." His voice was flat, no emotion running through the deep timbres. She closed her eyes, her hand squeezing his arm a little to give whatever comfort she could for the long ago agony.

"Daanae, our daughter, died first," he said after a long pause, and this time there was emotion in his voice. Anger. "For years I told myself it was because Laryssa hadn't heard the alarms. That she'd been asleep and the *Ovverta* had surprised her, but in my heart of hearts I always knew the truth. She ran. She ran and left our daughter to those monsters."

Tears hit the backs of Kenna's eyes, like hot needles. "I'm so sorry," she murmured. Just the idea was awful. He'd lived with that knowledge as well as the grief of their deaths.

He grunted and pulled her in closer against him to rest his chin on the top of her head. "You wouldn't run," he said suddenly. "You wouldn't have left a child to face that alone no matter how scared you were. You'd have died trying to protect any child, even if it wasn't yours."

Her breath caught in the back of her throat and she wriggled around to lie facing him. She searched his gaze, humbled at his words. At his belief in her.

"No, I would never leave a child in danger. Not while I had breath left in my body."

He looked pleased, as though her words had answered a question for him. "That's what I thought."

He leaned forward, intent in his eyes, and time stopped. This was it. He was going to kiss her. Finally. And... she froze. All her plans for what she was going to do when he finally made his move disappeared into the ether. All she could do was cling to his heavily muscled upper arms as he pulled her close.

His lips whispered over hers. A soft caress totally at odds with the ruthless warrior she knew he was, it was a mere press of his mouth against hers. She'd barely had time to register the warm smoothness of his lips before they were gone. She moaned in disappointment, crowding closer to kiss him. He chuckled, lips smiling against hers as he kissed her again.

This time it wasn't a soft brush. Nor was it tentative. This time, he pulled her closer with a strong arm around the back of her waist and claimed her lips like he owned them. She murmured, a soft sound in the back of her throat. His kiss was firm and dominant but not hard... simply leading them both to more pleasure. It held an edge of ruthlessness and experience that made a delicious shiver run all the way down her spine.

Eager for more, she parted her lips in invitation. He wasn't slow in taking her up on her offer with a deep rumble in the center of his chest that she felt more than heard. A large hand spread out over the back of her hips and pulled her up flush against him. Her breathing caught. He was hard, the solid bar of his cock pressing against her. More than that, he was *huge.*

She couldn't help the tiny sound in the back of her throat that was lost as his tongue swept past her lips. He invaded her mouth and teased her tongue with a sensuality she hadn't expected.

The kiss turned heated, filled with passion as he pressed her against the bed, half rolling over her and shoving a big hand into her hair. She whimpered and writhed against him. Her higher brain functions had shut down. There was only him, them, in the bed... and the heat and tension between them.

His knee pressed between her thighs so she parted them, sliding one foot up the back of his leg.

She panted when he broke from her lips to trail a line of kisses along the side of her neck. The cabin filled with her soft murmurs and his deeper, masculine sounds of pleasure, and the sheets slithered around them as they moved on the bed.

He lifted up to brace himself over her, the expression on his face one she couldn't read. Tilting her head in silent curiosity, she reached up to smooth gentle fingers over his cheek, tracing the line of his scar gently.

"I worried," he admitted gruffly, closing his eyes and turning his cheek against her touch, "that you wouldn't want a scarred and crippled old warrior."

"Who would that be then?" she teased softly, her heart going out to him that he thought he wasn't good enough. "As soon as I met you—"

Her words were cut off by a raucous screeching from the front of the cabin. She jumped, as much at the noise as the fact Xaan had vaulted out of bed. "What the hell is that?"

"Proximity alert," he called back. "*Trall...* There's a debris field that shouldn't be here. Get your ass up here and buckle in. I need to get us through this."

4

———

"The scans didn't mention any debris field..." Kenna frowned as she slid into the copilot's seat next to Xaan, her eyes narrowing. "This looks like ship debris, but I don't recall there being any battles out this way."

Xaan shook his head, his attention laser focused on the field in front of them as he navigated his way through it. It was easy to dodge the bigger bits of debris, but the smaller chunks could cause serious issues for the shielding. Shields were all well and good, but hit them often and hard enough and the generators would fail, especially on a little ship like this that wasn't configured with heavy shield grids for combat.

"No, and the readings say this isn't... wasn't a

Terran ship. Not being funny, but we can tell your ships a mile off. They're clunky and made from crude metals, not the usual hybrid alloys."

He risked a look at her. She was curled up in the copilot's seat again, wrapped in his jacket. It swamped her, making her look like a child playing dress up. He hadn't been prepared for the sight of her in his clothing, and a bolt of possessiveness and heat rolled through him so intensely he nearly cracked the controls in his hands.

The insistent bleep of an alarm snapped his head back around to the front screen. The computer-assisted flight control was good, but nothing beat actual eyes on the situation.

"If it's not Terran, whose is it?" she asked, but all he could think of as he brought them safely around a chunk of debris the size of a troop transport was the silky length of her legs sliding against his.

"Well... I can tell you what it's not. It's not supposed to be here," he added when he caught her curious look. "This is not a Terran ship in a Terran area. And there's no bit of it big enough for me to identify what type it was or who it belonged to."

"Can't you just... scan it? Like pick up minute variations in the alloys that tell you where it's from?"

He snorted. "No."

"Why not? You've got all these high-tech scanner thingies." She leaned forward to study the console in front of her. Currently it was showing energy outputs from the engines, rather than anything to do with the debris field, but she didn't know that because the screen was set to Latharian.

"High-tech sc—" he chuckled, shaking his head. "You've been watching too many of your species' fantasies... those 'films.' They're total rubbish."

"Hey! I like sci-fi films!" she huffed and folded the jacket around her more firmly. "So you can't tell anything about it? You could tell it wasn't Terran."

"That's because you people must just haul the metal out of the ground and pound it into shape with the mud still attached," he teased. "Scanners can give me a list of the likely hull composition. The problem is, most species in the galaxy use metals with similar compositions."

"Well... bugger." She sat back in the seat, a disappointed look on her face.

He could see the cogs working in the back of her mind and hid a smile. That was one of the things he liked so much about her. For all her insistence she was nothing more than a "grunt," which was apparently a name for the kind of warrior she was, she was highly intelligent and tenacious. Given a problem, she kept worrying at it, not giving up.

Even on him. He'd been aware of her interest in him since the first time they'd met. At first he'd put it down to simple curiosity. That she was as curious about the Lathar as they were about humanity. Before too long, though, it had become apparent that she wasn't just interested in the Lathar as a species, but him in particular.

And he'd been going to claim her. Before the battle that had nearly killed him.

The master healer had saved Xaan's life, but the road to recovery had been long and hard, and at some points it felt like he'd never recover full strength and movement in his damaged arm and shoulder. So he'd pushed her away, trying to make her lose interest in him. What could he have offered her but a lifetime with a bitter and crippled old warrior?

"Wait," she said suddenly. "You said you couldn't tell anything from the metals. Right?"

"I did." He wasn't sure where she was going with her question. Hadn't he just said that?

"Okay. But your sensors can tell the difference between a human and a Lathar, even though we're genetically related?"

"Of course. Easily." He grunted as he swung the ship between two large chunks of the debris, slipping through the rapidly narrowing gap. They were no longer recognizable as parts of a ship, the metal melted and twisted. What could render a ship into little more than scattered debris of molten metal lumps?

"Search for organic matter then." She practically bounced in her seat as she spoke, and he lost concentration for a moment to look at her. "What? It'll tell you who the ship belonged to. Won't it? I mean... a ship this size is not going to be automated."

"You..." he turned his attention back to the controls just in time to stop them ramming nose-first into another molten boulder, "are a *draanthing* genius. There should be some kind of organic matter in here somewhere."

The last boulder turned out to be the final large one. Seeing nothing else that would bother the shields, he put the ship back on autopilot and reconfigured the scanners to analyze any organic matter in the debris.

The results came back faster than he'd thought. He blinked in surprise at the readings.

"What?" she asked, seeing his expression. "What is it?"

He turned to her, a frown creasing his brow.

"It's... well, it *was*... a Latharian ship."

WHAT COULD DO this to a Latharian ship?

Kenna fell silent as they flew through the immense debris field. The first part had been the worst of it, with huge chunks of what looked like metallic rock big enough to crush the little ship between them, but the sheer size of the rest took her breath away.

Hours later they were still in the middle of it. The debris was smaller here, but even she could see it extended as far as she could see. What could cause such devastation that it scattered the remains of a ship over such a large area? Plus, Latharian ships were heavily armed and armored...

"There were no bodies," she realized suddenly.

And there hadn't been. Boulders the size of city blocks, but no bodies. Not one. She hadn't realized it at the time, but if a whole ship had been taken apart, there should be bodies. Surely?

"The level of destruction... The condition of the remains... The only thing that could have come anywhere near this is a *queshikall.* But—" Xaan shook his head. "Even a *queshikall* couldn't cause this level of devastation."

She wriggled to get more comfortable. She hadn't bothered to put pants on, so now her ass cheek was stuck to the leather. Carefully she eased to the side to free herself without making an unfortunate noise. Fart noises in front of a guy you were trying to impress? So not good.

"What's a *queshikall?*" she asked, pronouncing the unfamiliar word carefully.

"A bomb. One of the most powerful ones we use. Your people would call it a planet killer. But this is too expansive... no *queshikall* has a yield this big. We're entering the System Four Seven Alpha... Terran designation Delta Orellius."

She blinked as she looked through the front screen. When Daaynal had told them about the mission, she'd imagined the source of the problem to *be* something. Something physical or tangible. Perhaps a pirate outpost with high-yield generators running on illegal minerals. Or some mad scientist playing with energy-based technology he shouldn't have been.

But...

"There's nothing here. Nothing other than this anyway," she motioned at the debris around them.

Xaan was silent, his attention on the console in front of them. Figures and symbols she had no chance of understanding sped by on the screens. She looked at the big Latharian out of the corner of her eye. He was back to being the stone cold general, totally focused on the mission.

But she'd seen past the armor. He'd held her in his arms and talked about his late wife. It seemed like an odd conversation to have with a guy she was interested in, but it had actually reassured her he wasn't holding a torch for his late wife... mate.

An ex she could have dealt with, a ghost not so much. And his former mate had never called mating marks from his skin. So they couldn't have been soul mates.

"This here and here..." He stopped the cascade of information and pointed out two areas. "These don't make sense. These are the two levels we spotted on long-range scans. In this area they should be so low as to not even register, but here they're off the charts. It has to have something to do with the debris."

"Of a destroyed ship that shouldn't even be in

this area," she mused. "Could it have just, I dunno, gotten lost?"

He snorted, amusement on his face. "Out here? Not likely. This area of space is considered *vilarion*... hmmm, how would you say it? A space of uselessness...like land that is just dirt and ugly vegetation? Where unwanted things are put?"

"Wasteland?" She laughed. "You're telling me Terran space is considered wasteland?"

He nodded, a quirk on his lips. "Yes. That's why we didn't find you before. No one bothered to look here, and when it comes to space travel? You're infants. You've managed to get to the end of your garden and found some rocks to be excited about."

If she'd had a drink, she would have spat it out all over the screens in front of them. "Toddlers? Really?"

He nodded, a wicked little twinkle in his eyes, and opened his mouth to say something, but he was cut off as the console beeped and a new voice, distorted a little by static, filled the cabin.

"*...Please... if you can hear this... we've been attacked. Alien ships... need assistance.*"

The voice was female, frantic and speaking in English. Her gaze collided with Xaan's.

"There are colonies out here. What if whatever did this..." She waved at the debris field. "Attacked them as well? We have to go and look. Check they're okay."

He nodded, his expression grim as his hands flew over the console. "The signal is coming from a smaller system not far from here. It won't take us long." He smiled at her wryly. "Another 'hold that thought' I'm afraid."

"No problem." She'd assumed that and people in trouble definitely took precedence. The deepened lines at the corners of his lips and the expression in his eyes caught her attention. "Something's bothering you about this. Isn't it? Talk to me."

He shook his head. "I don't know what it is, but this doesn't add up. That was a Lathar ship in an area it shouldn't have been. It wasn't an imperial one, so that just leaves Purists or..."

Her breath caught at the word. The Purist faction within Latharian society was fanatical and violent. Since the discovery of humanity, they'd done everything they could to attack or kill the human women they could get to. They'd attacked her friend Cat's wedding, tried to kill her other friend Jess while she was pregnant and take the child for sacrifice... They were not nice people. The idea of them being anywhere *near* human space sent shivers down her spine.

She consoled herself with the thought that, had it been a purist ship, it was destroyed. No survivors.

"Or?" she asked, realizing he'd been about to offer a second option.

"Or pirates."

She blinked and ran the word through her head again to be sure he'd said what she'd thought.

"Pirates?" She laughed. This got better and better. "Seriously? Like space pirates?"

"Yes... why is that funny?" Xaan didn't seem to see the funny side so she gave up. Explaining the idea of a swashbuckling space pirate was beyond her right now. "The C'Vaal are highly dangerous and capable warriors. Their leader was an imperial prince, but they had a difference of opinion with Daaynal's father, so they were given territory in the Denair expanse. If they've decided to increase their territory, humanity could be in *real* trouble."

He shook his head. "I need to get a message through this interference to the fleet. Warn them of a possible C'Vaal presence. Go get dressed. We'll be at the source of that distress call before long."

She slid out of the copilot's seat, only for him to stop her with a big hand on her thigh. It slid up to her hip, the touch possessive, and left tingles chasing over her skin. Her breathing caught as she looked into his eyes, the blue rendered stormy and dark.

"But make no mistake, *kelarris,* I intend to collect on those held thoughts soon."

5

*E*ven after months living among them, Latharian technology could still surprise Kenna occasionally.

"It looks exactly like a Terran trader ship," she exclaimed in surprise, turning to Xaan. They'd reached the surface without incident, landing a short distance away from the only settlement on the planet, and were now looking back at the ship from a small rise nearby. The ship had somehow managed to conceal it's non-Terran origin so well that even she would have been fooled.

Xaan looked different as well, his eyes altered somehow to look human. Dressed in Terran clothing he looked like the archetype of a rough-neck trader, one of the few insane enough to eek out a living in the outer systems. Away from the control of any bureaucratical oversight, they lived on the fringes of society "exploring" the edges of known space and selling whatever they found. Occasionally it was something useful that the scientific community went gaga over. Sometimes it blew their ships up. Such was the nature of meddling with shit you didn't understand.

"How did you do that?" she asked, indicating both his eyes and the ship.

"Magic."

He grinned, a twinkle of amusement in his eyes. They looked odd with round pupils like hers, she realized. She'd gotten used to him with vertical pupils.

"Magic, my ass," she growled. "I knew I shouldn't have given you access to all those old films. You'll be calling yourself Merlin next."

He looked at her oddly. "I do have M'rlin blood on my mother's side. A long way back."

"Oh, you are *kidding* me. Merlin was real?"

She'd stopped walking, looking at him in utter surprise. "He's just a myth. A legend. They never found *any* evidence he and his magic were real."

He shrugged as she hurried to catch up with

him, his long legs eating up the distance toward the settlement they'd scanned from space.

"Maybe not, but if you with your technology could go back in time, you'd appear to be a god to your ancestors. Wouldn't you?"

"Huh. Yeah, I guess so. Or sorcerers at the very least."

Silence fell between them as they walked, the heather colored grasses brushing her ankles. Taking a deep breath, she savored the sweet-smelling air. It wasn't as pleasant and fragrant as Lathar Prime, but it was still a welcome relief after weeks traveling aboard a star-ship. Recycled air was perfectly safe, but it was flat and dead. Her lungs could tell the difference.

She was dressed very much the same as Xaan was, like a trader, which was no surprise as their cover was a married couple. She hadn't argued when he'd suggested it, liking the idea of the fantasy... the idea of being his wife. So she snuck her hand into his as they walked, smiling at his surprised little look and then melting inside when he lifted her hand to place a soft kiss on the back of her knuckles.

They reached another, higher rise and the settlement came into view beneath them. She paused for a moment and took in the view. It was idyllic with cloud-topped mountains to the north, rolling hills surrounding it, and what looked like a warm sea to the south.

"I grew up on a colony. Not like this one," she commented. "This is way nicer than where I came from. I'm from the Epsilon quadrant. Now *that* is a wasteland. It's the ass-end of beyond. I have no idea why they put a colony there. Nothing but fucking dirt and rocks. And Anarin Root—it's the colony's main export."

They started down the incline, watching their footing. Every so often Xaan's grip tightened on her hand to help her down a steeper bit. She didn't need the help since she was accustomed to route marches and combat over rough terrain, but it was nice to let him look after her.

"Anarin Root? Never heard of it."

She shrugged. "You won't, not unless you're a foodie. They use it in fancy-shmancy restaurants. It's a bastard to harvest though. It's got thick bark and the root trails are barbed. We fry it off and dip it in sugar. Tastes awesome that way."

Shouts from up ahead warned them that they'd been seen, and within a few minutes a group headed toward them from the front gates of the settlement. Like most colonies, it had been built within a fortified wall as protection for the colonists in a potentially hostile environment.

"They're armed." Xaan's voice was low, pitched so only she could hear. "Look a little twitchy."

His eyesight was better than hers, so it took another thirty seconds or so for her to make out the tight expressions on their faces and the fact fingers were way too close to triggers for her liking.

"Keep it calm," she advised, her body language relaxed.

Xaan grunted. "I don't like it. They're too hostile."

"No, it's okay." She leaned closer to him for reassurance but didn't reach out again to take his hand. Any movement on her part might be mistaken for something else by the group approaching. "It's perfectly normal. They're bound to be a little wary of visitors if they've been attacked."

He just grunted, but she could feel the tension and displeasure rolling off him in waves.

The colony itself didn't show any signs of damage, she noted, plastering a wide smile on her lips as the armed group approached them. There were six, four men and two women. Two walked directly toward them while the remaining four spread out, staying back. Sensible. Kenna nodded to herself in approval at the way they acted. Someone, somewhere, had taught these people the basics of field movement and it showed.

"Hey there!" she called out, automatically slipping into the agreeable persona she'd been taught to adopt when dealing with locals. No sunglasses, big smile. It all made a difference in how people saw her and reacted. "We got your distress call and thought we'd swing on by and make sure you guys were all right."

She'd also dropped back into the lazy drawl of a colonist born and bred. It had been something she'd tried to eradicate in her speech during her service, but it didn't take but a moment for her to call it back up.

"Hey yourselves." The spokesperson was one of the women, a tall, sparse woman with grey-streaked blonde hair scraped back off her face into a thin plait over her shoulder. "We didn't see you land or hear your reply."

Kenna shrugged, pretending not to notice that the woman's finger hadn't moved from her trigger guard.

"Got some weirdness in the upper atmosphere, so we had to set down a ways back there." She waved vaguely behind them. "Then it was the old leather personnel carriers to get us over here. We got medical supplies onboard if you guys need 'em," she added, her voice filled with concern.

The woman relaxed a little, giving them a little smile as her gaze flicked over them. It was a smile that got broader as she looked at Xaan. Kenna bit back her instinctive growl at the woman's obvious interest in the big, handsome pretend-trader.

"I'm Helen," she said abruptly and then nodded to the other five members of her team. "Chloe, James, Korric, Geoff and Trent."

"Pleasure to meet you all," Xaan said, surprising her by answering first, in perfect English with a drawl to match hers. "I'm Steve Renner. My wife, Suzie."

Kenna plastered a smile over her face to hide her surprise. They hadn't even discussed names, and obviously he couldn't use his own. But... Steve? She didn't think she'd ever met anyone *less* like a Steve than Xaan. And where had he picked up a colony-hick accent?

Helen's smile cooled a little at the revealed relationship between Kenna and Xaan and she whistled sharply.

"Come on then, guys, let's get our guests back inside the walls before night falls. You do not want to be out here after dark," she told them as they started to walk back to the settlement. "There's some real nasty local critters that'll snack on your spine before you even realized they've ripped it from your body."

Kenna shuddered and dropped into step. Even with all her military training and one of the most dangerous creatures in the universe at her side, with a warning like that, she knew better than to want to be outside the walls after nightfall.

"WELCOME, WELCOME!"

They'd barely walked into the main compound, the heavy metal gates scraping shut behind them, when a man strode toward them with a wide smile on his face. He was tall and wiry, his clothes as sun-worn and patched as Helen's group.

"This is Dex, our leader," Helen informed them. "Dex, this is Steve and Suzie Renner. They heard our distress call and came to help us."

"Is that so?" Dex shook their hands enthusiastically, the wide smile still in place. "That's awesome. I can't thank you enough. We've been having some... issues."

"Yeah. We were a couple of systems over and picked up your signal," Xaan replied, letting go of the man's hand quickly. He concealed his distrust well, but Kenna *knew* him. He wasn't just uncomfortable, which was perfectly understandable surrounded by a species not his own, he didn't trust the colonists. Not one bit. "It was a bit patchy though. We weren't sure how old it was... or what state you'd be in when we got here..."

He looked around, obviously noting as Kenna had, that the settlement looked okay. There was no damage to any of the structures. All in all, it didn't look like a colony that had suffered an attack. To the contrary, it looked like it was thriving.

"Yeah, we've been having some trouble getting the signal out. Interference in the upper atmosphere..." Dex explained, casting a frowning look upward as though the clear sky above them was the culprit. His pale blue eyes latched on to them again. "Had a spate of attacks a week or so ago. Ships the like of which we'd never seen before buzzing the fields. Obviously attack drones from those Lathar aliens that have been in the newsfeeds recently. Attacking bases and kidnapping people."

Kenna frowned. This far out, the news they got must be months old. So, they didn't know the Lathar were in talks with the Terran government now. They still thought of them as the enemy.

"Attack drones?" Xaan frowned. "And you didn't see a main ship, just the drones?"

Dex shook his head, motioning for them to follow him. As they turned, Kenna caught Xaan's eye. The big Latharian shook his head slightly.

The Lathar didn't use attack drones. They dropped troops and combat bots onto the ground or flew bigger fighter jets. She'd never heard of or seen flying attack bots. Whoever it was, it wasn't the Lathar. She'd already guessed that. With their technology and combat capability, if they'd attacked this place, it wouldn't still be standing.

"Nope. Just the blasted drones. Initially we thought they were just surveying us to see what assets we had on the planet and then they'd send in a full-scale attack. But... we're a small colony. We don't have anything here they'd be interested in, so the big attack never came."

"Sounds like you had a lucky escape," Kenna commented as they stepped out of the sun and into the cool interior of the main colony building.

Like most colonies, it was built to a standard design. An extruded plasticrete central building, hexagonal in shape, housed all the main facilities, with tunnel-like corridors off to other smaller buildings. As the colony grew in size, more and more corridors and buildings could be added until it resembled a huge rabbit warren.

From the size and complexity of the place, the settlement wasn't that old. Only a couple of years at the most. Odd. This far out she would have expected the colony to have been at least in its sixth decade.

"They didn't do any damage then?" she asked, scanning the interior of the main building with a quick eye.

She kept her expression neutral, not revealing she knew anything about what she was looking at. But... the internal structure of the main building was as she'd expected, with some of the phase one room dividers still in place.

Colonies were designed around the main building. During their first years everyone lived together, with the big space sectioned off with dividers and low decks to provide living and storage space around the edges. The middle section was left for communal use, with washrooms and facilities set at the back.

Most of the personal spaces were gone. Some looked like they had been converted into offices, but a few remained, as did the communal kitchen and washrooms. All as she'd expect for a colony that hadn't jumped all the way to phase two yet.

"Not to the buildings. But..." Dex sighed heavily, running a hand through his close-cropped hair. "We lost two field workers. Slaughtered by the drones."

Kenna blinked in surprise. "Slaughtered?"

"What do you mean... slaughtered?" Xaan asked, putting an arm around her waist and pulling her close protectively.

"Best I show you."

Dex's face was grim as he led them toward one of the many doors off the main hall. They walked down a short corridor, the plasticrete roof translucent in sections to allow the light through. Strip lighting ran in beads along the walls at ankle height.

A sharp right turn later, they emerged into a medical bay with sterile metal surfaces and harsh lights. The low hum of generators filled the room, powering the two refrigeration units against one wall, right next to a couple of mortuary cabinets. Each had four doors.

Dex walked over to the one nearest the door, stopping as he reached for the handle of the second door from the bottom. He looked over his shoulder at Xaan. "You might want your wife to leave the room," he warned. "This is... not for the faint of heart."

Xaan shook his head, casting her a quick glance.

"Oh, my Suzie's a tough nut. She'll be fine. I promise."

"Aright," Dex shrugged. "But don't say I didn't warn you."

He pulled the door open and slid the drawer out. Despite all her military training, Kenna gasped and covered her mouth. A man lay on the metal tray. At least, he looked like a man from the neck and shoulders up. Below that...

Her eyes widened as her gaze trailed down his body. Or what was left of it. It looked like he'd been in some industrial accident. One leg below the knee was gone and the stump looked like it had been chewed on. Deep slashes cut into the thighs, carrying on into the torso. Some were so close together the flesh was little more than chum. There was a big indentation on the left side of the chest where a large portion was missing.

"The other one is worse. I won't show you her," Dex said quietly, stepping back to allow Xaan to step up and examine the body. Kenna stayed safely back. She had a strong stomach, yes, any marine had. But there were some states no one ever needed to see a body in. It was the stuff nightmares were made of. She blinked, clearing her mind of blast and combat injuries she'd seen and breathing deeply to help herself relax. The lights were way too bright in here, she told herself.

It didn't help. The deep breath brought the smell of death into her lungs and her body rebelled, threatening to bring back up the little she'd eaten today.

"I'm sorry. I need to get some air," she muttered and fled.

6

*D*ex and Xaan found her kicking her heels outside a few minutes later. Kenna looked up as the big Latharian strode out of the main hall, his expression grim as he scanned the surroundings. Then tension in his shoulders eased, his blue eyes filling with warmth as he walked over to her.

"You okay, love?" he asked, sliding a hand around the back of her waist to pull her close.

"Yeah. I will be. I just need a moment."

She nestled against his larger body, her forehead resting against his shoulder, and closed her eyes for a moment. He dropped a kiss on the top of her head.

"You take as long as you need. I'm not going anywhere."

She nodded and savored the moment. Just being near him calmed her down and gave her strength. The fact that he'd been concerned and obviously didn't like the fact they'd been separated, even for such a short period, warmed her heart. The sensible part of her, the marine part, wanted to say it was because they were a unit, albeit a unit of just two, behind enemy lines. Splitting up wasn't sensible. But she knew better. His concern was personal, and, from the way he held her... possessive.

"I'm sorry," she murmured, aware that Dex was watching them from the doorway. "I thought I could handle that. But..." She broke off and buried her face against his chest. "It was just too much."

"Hey, hey, you don't need to apologize to me."

Strong fingers at the back of her neck tilted her head up and she met Xaan's concerned eyes. Bless him, he really *was* worried about her. Worried that she'd been overset by what she'd seen for all of two point four seconds before he clocked the amusement buried deep in the backs of her eyes. The tiny muscle at the corner of his lips quirked and she knew he was onto her act. The tough and mean on the outside, sensitive marshmallow inside trader woman who'd developed her persona to survive in the harsh reality of the outer systems.

"It's all good. I promise," he murmured, playing up his part as her strong, brooding but reliable husband. Then he leaned down to brush his lips over hers and all thought of their cover story hightailed it over the horizon.

She parted her lips with a small murmur of invitation, shivering as his tongue brushed against her lower lip. Once. Twice. Then he invaded her mouth, his hold on her tightening as he deepened the kiss. She gripped the front of his jacket, holding him to her as she kissed him back. Heat rose between them, an instant inferno that set her heart racing and need coursing through her veins.

"Oh for heaven's sake, get a room," a female voice yelled at them good-naturedly and they broke apart. Kenna grinned at the woman who'd called out, one of a group of colonists heading into the main hall.

"It's beginning to get dark," Dex commented as he approached, nodding up at the darkening sky. "You won't want to return to your ship until morning, not with what's out there. You're more than welcome to spend the night here. I'll have a room made up for you."

Her fingers tightened on the lapels of Xaan's jacket as he stiffened, and she knew he was about to argue that they could make it. She leaned against him in warning. While a Latharian warrior would think nothing of hightailing it back through hostile territory, the traders they were pretending to be would never risk it.

"Thank you," she replied with a nod. "That's most kind of you."

"No problem at all. Our pleasure. Feel free to head on into the hall. The evening meal should be serving soon." Dex paused for a moment, frowning as he looked directly at Kenna. "Are you sure we've never met? You look awfully familiar."

"I get that a lot." She gave a little smile. "Just have one of those faces, I guess. No, we've never met. Steve and I have never been this far out before."

"Huh. Odd. Anyway, you'll have to excuse me. I need to brief the night watch." As he spoke, spotlights snapped on around the perimeter wall, guards stationed at each and patrolling the high catwalks.

"Of course. We wouldn't want to keep you from such an important task." Xaan smiled, but the expression didn't reach his eyes and they watched as the colony leader walked away.

"What's gotten into you?" Kenna hissed in an

undertone as they turned toward the main hall. If he carried on like this, Dex would smell a rat.

Xaan's hand tightened warningly around hers. "Not here. Later."

She gave a small nod, allowing him to lead her into the main hall. The main space had been filled with tables and chairs. The smell of something good wafted through the air from the kitchens now visible through open hatches in one set of dividers.

"Hey! Welcome! Feel free to grab a seat where you can," someone called out from the other side of the room. It was already half full, workers having come in while they were in the medical bay. Kenna cast a glance over them. Definitely field workers, which up Dex's story about the attack.

"Thanks, will do!" she called out in reply.

They were subjected to curious looks as they made their way to an empty table at the back of the room. A woman broke away from the serving hatch to put two plates loaded with stew in front of them.

"Hey, how comes I don't get table service, Maggie?" a male voice called out. "That's downright favoritism, that is!"

"You shut your cake-hole, Jeremiah!" Maggie shot back with a laugh. "Them's guests. You ain't.

Now get back to eatin' your chow before Elias there snags it from under that big nose of yours!"

She added a basket filled with thick cut bread to the table. "Husbands," she grinned at Kenna. "Can't live with 'em, can't bury them under the lettuce patch...am I right?"

Kenna chuckled, shooting a glance at Xaan. He frustrated her so much at times she'd happily bury him under the lettuce. In a totally affectionate way, of course.

Something was definitely up with him though. The lines at the corners of his mouth betrayed his tension. She couldn't imagine it was because he was a Lathar alone in the midst of humans. No one here, even her, was a threat to a fully trained and experienced warrior. So, it was something else.

What had he seen that she hadn't? Other than the inconsistencies about the age of the colony, which could be explained away by a longer route or technical difficulties before they landed, there was nothing out of the ordinary for this kind of settlement.

They ate in silence, but that didn't mean Kenna's mind was idle. She watched the people around them out of the corner of her eye, noting everyone as they came, ate, and went. Some to sleep, while others looked like they were pulling a night shift. Were they still hot-bedding? One shelter or room shared by two or three shifts, one sleeping while the other two were at work or recreation. Surely they'd already grown past that, though?

Xaan leaned forward after a while, his voice low as he spoke, "These family groups appear to be different to the norm for your species."

"Huh? What do you mean?" His question had caught her by surprise and stalled her observation of a girl in the kitchens. Unlike the others, she seemed sullen and quiet, not speaking to or making eye contact with anyone.

Xaan nodded to a group a couple of tables away. A large man was laughing, sharing a joke with the women sitting around him, several children either on laps or running around the group playing. From the similarities of their facial features, they were obviously closely related.

"Ah. Multiple marriage is common out here," she told him quietly. "Larger group to take care of the children. Makes it easier on all involved. It's usually one man with multiple wives, but sometimes it occurs the other way as well."

She flicked a glance toward a quiet group nearer the door where a woman sat surrounded by three men. Their body language was incredibly possessive, so she didn't need the glint of rings on their fingers to clue her in. Must be newly married as well by the tension swirling around them.

"Your males share women?" Xaan asked in surprise. "That occasionally happens with us as well, but it's rare. I don't know of any male who would be selfish enough to take more than one woman as mate, though. How would he cope with the needs of so many women without someone being neglected?" He looked offended at the very thought. "That would not be right at all."

She suppressed a wry snort. "And there you have the problem with human men in a nutshell. Some believe they're god's gift to women. Hence the invention of the dick pic."

"A god's gift?" he looked confused. "What did your females do to offend a god that he would grant them such a... dubious gift? What is a 'dick pic'? Your males call their genit..." He broke off, looking horrified. "Is that— Do you mean what I think you mean?"

"Yeah. They send a picture of their junk and think it's seductive." She couldn't help it. She burst out laughing. "Oh, you are just comedy gold. But no, you're right. We must have done something way back when to deserve it."

Xaan rumbled in the back of his throat and dug into his stew. "Your males are idiots if you ask me. They've got things all the wrong way around."

"No arguments from me on that," Kenna murmured in reply, still watching the quiet girl behind the counter as she ate. She looked to be a teenager, thin, with lanky, dark hair. When she wiped her hands and took off her apron, Kenna slid out of her seat, murmuring to Xaan, "Back in a moment."

She ducked through the door nearest to the kitchens, mouthing "ladies" to Maggie on the way and getting a thumbs up. Good, she'd guessed right on the location of the facilities then. It was the work of a moment to find the right restroom and yes, the other stall was occupied.

Quickly going about her business, Kenna stepped back out of her stall afterward to find the girl washing her hands. She smiled as she stepped up to the sink next to her and snapped the water on.

"Hey. How's it going?"

The girl flicked her a nervous glance and gave a small sound in reply. It could have been teenager for hi or it could have been a grunt. Kenna wasn't sure which.

"Nice planet you got. Have you been here long?" she asked, washing her hands. "Do you like it here?"

"She likes it just fine. Don't you, Ava?" a hard voice asked from the doorway. "What have you been told about bothering people?"

It was the older woman who'd been working in the kitchen. Not Maggie, who was all smiles, but a taller, wiry woman with a face like a bulldog chewing a wasp. Instantly the hackles went up on the back of Kenna's neck, her instincts warning her to be careful around this one.

Ava whirled around, her expression pale and defensive. "I weren't talking to her. She were doin' the talking!" she exclaimed and fled, banging through the door where the older woman stood.

"I wouldn't pay attention to anything that one says," Bulldog-face said, crossing her arms over her flat chest and glaring at Kenna. "Ungrateful brat with a head full of made-up shite she likes to pedal to anyone that'll listen."

"No problem. I was only saying hi anyway, being polite."

Kenna dried off her hands and made to move past. She kept her expression bland and polite when it looked like the other woman was considering blocking her path, but her entire body was on alert. If she made one move that looked threatening, Kenna was ready for it.

For all that she was concealing her military training and background, something in the way she moved or the look in her eyes must have warned Bulldog-face because she dropped her gaze and moved to the side. Kenna murmured her thanks and left the washroom without a backward glance.

"What happened?" Xaan asked, pushing the last slice of bread over as she sat back down. "The young female from the kitchens came out of there like a stabbed *sukazin.*"

"Trouble in paradise I think," Kenna mused in a low voice and then shrugged as she realized Maggie was watching them. "Perhaps just teenage trouble. You know what girls that age are like."

"It ain't much, but it's one of the better rooms." Maggie bustled ahead of them down one of the warren-like corridors of the colony's main structure and opened a low door. Behind it was a small bedroom, mostly dominated by the bed under the skyport window. "Bedding's just out the scrubber, so excuse the smell. It'll fade off before morning and..." she grinned and winked at Kenna. "Guy lookin' like that, well, I figure you'll be too busy to notice... know what I mean?"

Kenna chuckled, her cheeks reddening. "I'm sure we won't notice the smell. It's been a long day..."

"Yeah, yeah..." The big, cheerful woman obviously didn't believe a word she said, eyeing Xaan with an appreciative grin. "Whatever you say, hon."

She moved to open another door. It stuck halfway, and she gave it a practiced kick on the bottom corner. Kenna's grin broadened a little at the little reminder of home. Plasticrete often swelled in the heat, so doors in the personal spaces caught a lot.

"Washroom's through here. Three-minute limit on the shower per person. Even bein' a guest don't get you no more hot water'n that I'm afraid. Breakfast is at seven. Be there early if you want feedin' cause this lot'll clean me out faster'n a pack of rats. Well then, I'll leave you two young 'uns to it! Don't do anything I wouldn't do!" She winked and headed for the door.

"Thank you so much for your hospitality, Maggie. Good night," Kenna said, closing the door behind her as she left. She leaned against it to look at Xaan.

"What on earth's gotten into you?" she demanded. He was acting well out of character. Like a cat on a hot tin roof.

He shook his head, fishing something out of his pocket and setting it on the bedside cabinet. It looked like a standard personal communicator and she wondered for a moment who he'd lifted it off. But then he pressed a button on the side. Lights erupted from the top of the device, spreading out into a grid that covered the ceiling, flowed down the walls to outline the window and doors, and then created a chessboard floor. Three spots flared brightly, two in the corners of the ceiling and the lamp by the bed.

Xaan fiddled with the device. The spots and the grid disappeared with a snap.

"Okay, we're good," Xaan straightened up, dropping the trader accent. "That's blocked the mics they have in here."

"They *bugged* us?" She blinked but then laughed and shook her head. "Xaan, this is a backwater colony. They're not known for their high-stakes espionage."

He folded his arms over his broad chest, his

expression forbidding. Before he spoke, he covered his mouth with his hand, not enough to muffle his voice, but to conceal his lips she realized. "Stay by the door, you're out of sight of the cameras. Maybe not, but they were listening to us and I don't trust them."

She folded her arms as well, mirroring his posture. "Maybe they are. Perhaps they think we're here scouting for weaknesses. Pirates *are* known in this area and a colony like this? Easy pickings for a scavenger group."

He shook his head. "I don't think it's that. Something feels wrong here."

She arched her eyebrow. "Are you sure that's not just because they're human? You've only ever dealt with human females before. Not males."

His expression didn't change. "You think I am that easily led by my emotions?"

The temperature in the room dropped a couple of degrees.

"No." Kenna didn't raise her voice, the center of her chest aching. He didn't trust humans. That was plain to see. So where did that leave them? "I think you're in a new situation and you don't like it. A few of us? That's a different matter than dealing with a whole colony where you're the odd one out."

"You don't know anything about me, Kenna," he said in a low, half-growl, his eyes flashing dangerously. "You know what you've been told, or what you've managed to glean. This is not the first time I've been on my own amongst others not my own kind."

"Oh? Did you take an instant dislike to them as well?" Her words were sharp, but to the point. "Because that's what it seems like to me. I haven't been among many of my own kind for months... and you start behaving like a jerk as soon as we are."

He was across the room before she registered the movement, slamming a hand into the door by her head. Anger heated his eyes as he bit out, "So that's it, is it? You prefer your own kind? Probably prefer a human male as well. Dex probably."

She blinked, blindsided by his anger and his assumption. "Dex? No! *God* no," she exclaimed and then reached for him. "Xaan... stop, just stop. I don't want a human male. I want you. Okay?"

He sighed and pulled her close, wrapping her up in his strong arms. "I'm sorry," he whispered, his lips pressed against her hair. "I see you looking at them, smiling at them... and I want to kill them, every single one, so I can keep all your smiles for myself."

His growl made her chuckle. "Please don't kill all

the colonists just because I smiled at them. That wouldn't give the right impression of the Lathar at all. Would it?"

He grumbled in the back of his throat, but he was smiling as he pulled her away from the door and ushered her toward the washroom. "Go get ready for bed. And keep the door shut," he warned her. "I don't want anyone spying on you."

"Aye aye, Captain Renner, sir!" She gave him a wink and a smart salute and then disappeared into the bathroom and shut the door behind her as ordered.

7

---

*S*leeping with Kenna in his arms had affected Xaan more than he'd thought it would. It had both soothed his soul to hold her close as she slept and kept him awake half the night because of the temptation of her slender, curvy body pressed against his. But other than a heated kiss he'd ruthlessly kept under control before they'd slept, he'd behaved himself.

Even though he'd wanted nothing more than to roll her over and pin her beneath him, kiss her until she moaned and writhed under him, he hadn't. Bracing his hands against the washbasin in the tiny washroom off the bedroom, he battled the instinctive reaction of his body to the idea. He battled the need to walk back into the bedroom and tumble her down onto the bed so he could claim her.

No. No way.

He would not take his mate hurriedly with others watching them. She deserved better. She deserved romance and time for them to get to know each other physically. She deserved all his attention as he discovered what she liked, what made her squirm, and what made her scream in pleasure. And he *would* make her scream—time and time again as he made her come and gave her pleasure.

"I could get used to this view in the morning."

Her voice reached him from the bedroom and he turned to smile over his shoulder. Kenna was still in bed, lying on her side wrapped up in all the blankets as she watched him.

"Good," he threw back, loving the possessive little gleam in her eyes. She was everything he wanted in a woman—fierce and loyal. He couldn't wait to get back to the ship so he could claim her as his own finally. "Because you'll have to."

Kenna frowned and sat up, something in the main room catching her attention.

"What is it?" he asked as she slid out from under the covers.

"Someone just pushed something under the door."

He stepped out of the washroom to find her with a piece of paper in her hand. She looked up and held it out to him silently. A message was scrawled in marker across the dirty cream surface.

Trust no one.

THE MESSAGE STUCK with Xaan all the way through breakfast, and Kenna had to hiss to remind him not to glare at people and blow their cover. He was forced to get ahold of himself and focus on the mission. It was a task when all he wanted to do was grab Kenna and fight his way out of there.

This distraction was new and not altogether welcome. Even though he'd been mated before, he'd never reacted like this, had this loss of focus on a mission. But then, Laryssa hadn't been a warrior like Kenna. She'd always remained at home, safely. Apart from that final time...

He pulled his mind away from the memory but not because it had any power to hurt him, only because he needed to focus on their mission. Namely getting himself and Kenna out of here. Now they'd checked that the colony wasn't in danger, and it didn't appear to be, there was no need for them to remain.

Still, something about those bodies bothered him. The wounding patterns seemed familiar somehow. But... the colonists kept on about predators in the area, so it could easily have been one of them.

He shook it off and shoveled something Kenna had called "eggs" into his mouth. It was weird, rubbery stuff that tasted artificial. He'd much rather have field cake—standard Latharian rations that gave a warrior all his nutritional needs for the day and kicked his metabolism into high gear.

He flicked a glance at Kenna, who was demolishing some sticky, gooey confection with relish. He suspected if he *did* have field cake, he wouldn't be the one to eat it. It hadn't escaped anyone's notice that the human women were inordinately fond of what they called "chocolate cake," which was what they'd dubbed field rations.

"Hey guys," Dex dropped into the seat next to Xaan. "Did you sleep okay?"

Kenna smiled at the guy and Xaan glowered for a moment, wanting to drive his elbow into Dex's throat and crush his windpipe. Or maybe his nose and spread it all over his face. *Draanthic* wouldn't get her smiles then.

"Yeah. We slept well thanks," he rumbled, getting his murderous impulses under control. Dex irritated him beyond measure. He tried to tell himself it was because something about the guy wasn't on the level, but could Kenna be right? Could he mistrust the guy simply because he was human and he'd considered him a rival for her affections? She had a valid point that none of them had had much interaction with the males of her species. He grumbled to himself. And the ones he'd had anything to do with before this had proved to be complete and utter *trallshit.*

But there *had* been spy cams in their room. It might just be something voyeuristic, and to be honest, he couldn't blame any male wanting to get a closer look at Kenna. But she was *his.* Quickly he batted the fury down again.

"Much obliged to you for the room and board, but since you ain't in no danger," he said, sticking to the dialect he'd observed Kenna and some of the others use. "Then we'll be getting on our way today. Got some cargo we need to move further into civilized space."

"Sure, sure... Understand totally." Dex nodded, a

mug of steaming coffee in his hands. They were thin and callused like Xaan's. A worker's hands. "Thanks for dropping in on us. I have to ask, though. You said you were an engineer?"

He hadn't, but a warning kick from Kenna under the table had him nodding. "Of a sort, yeah. Why? What's up?"

"Could do with a hand getting that radio up and running. Just in case those aliens come back again."

He exchanged glances with Kenna. It wasn't an unreasonable request and, seriously, how long would it take him? He hadn't been a science officer for years, but he'd never forgotten his training and primary discipline. And given what he'd seen of the colony, they were years behind the central system Terrans, so their primitive technology should be easy to fix.

"Yeah. Sure." He nodded, finishing up the eggs. They weren't that bad. Especially with the spicy sauce all over them. "I'll take a look."

"Cool, that would be awesome! Meet us out front when you're done here, and we'll head out to the booster towers. We've isolated the problem to one of them."

Twenty minutes later, Xaan and Kenna stood outside in the main square as the work teams started to assemble. Most were ready to head out into the fields, and he wondered what kind of crops they grew. The question was answered a moment later, at least in part, when Kenna gasped and stopped a woman walking by them.

"Is that a *goojan* berry basket?" she asked, eagerness written all over her beautiful face.

"Errr, yeah," the woman replied, flicking quick glances at the pair of them. "We got a patch over the other side of the valley, near a small stream."

Kenna was all smiles. "I *love goojan* berries."

"You'll have to head out with Liz and her group," Dex broke in, appearing at Xaan's side. "They'll be back at lunch so that gives Steve here plenty of time to look at the radio issue."

He didn't want them to split up, but at the look of delight and anticipation on his beautiful soon-to-be-mate's face he didn't have the heart to tell her no. It would take him a while to trek with Dex out to the towers, fix whatever was wrong and get back anyway. Plenty enough time for her to go pick as many berries as she wanted.

"You head out, love," he said, leaning down to

kiss her on the forehead. "Make sure not to eat more than you pick though."

She chuckled and nodded. "Promise. See you at lunch."

"You two been married long?" Dex asked as Xaan watched Kenna walk off to join the berry-picking group. He told himself it was purely professional, making sure a member of his team was okay, but even he didn't believe that. No, he outright ogled her slender figure and shapely ass, highlighted in the cargo pants she wore, as she walked away.

"Couple of years now," he replied, looking at the other man. "Why?"

Dex chuckled. "Didn't think it was that long. You still look at her like you want to rip her clothes off and fuck her right now."

Xaan grunted, not liking the human linking Kenna and fucking in the same thought. "You wanted me to look at this radio?"

WITHIN A FEW MINUTES XAAN, Dex and two others left the compound. Xaan had raised his eyebrow at the high-powered rifles the two men held, more combat weapons than something he'd expect a colony to use for hunting. Dex spotted his look.

"Got some nasty predators in the area. Pays to be prepared," he said, patting his sidearm. "This is Billy and Rob. They'll be coming with us."

It was a sensible precaution, so Xaan let it go, even if he did have the sneaking feeling the guards were keeping more of an eye on him rather than on the surroundings while Dex kept checking his personal communicator like it held the secrets of life itself.

The planet itself was pleasant—the kind of place he might have brought Kenna for a romantic getaway. They were headed northeast so the view ahead was filled with rolling hills and forests. The sky was clear and more toward the blue spectrum, the air pleasant. From the pictures he'd seen, the place could pass as Earth, apart from the purple grass and fauna. Although, it made sense that humans would seek out planets like their home... which in turn was similar to Lathar Prime. Strange how it all came full circle.

As he walked, he allowed his mind to fill with thoughts of Kenna again. Her softly worded admission last night that she wanted him, not a human mate, had eased a knot inside he hadn't known was there. He realized he'd been worried that once back amongst her own kind she wouldn't want to leave. She wouldn't want him, a scarred veteran warrior from another race with an adult son, anymore.

He'd spent time reviewing the files they'd gleaned from the base they'd taken Kenna and her friends from. He'd seen the entertainment files. Art imitated life and in most of their romantic dealings, it seemed human females mostly favored younger males. Young, fit and stupid if what he'd seen was typical.

The males in these "rom-coms" seemed to be clueless with females, only realizing the perfect female was right there after events forced them to. They'd only proved to him that human males weren't fit to reproduce. Any Latharian warrior would have taken one look at the female and done everything he could to claim her. None of this commitment-phobic behavior that almost caused the female to walk away forever.

He wasn't young, but he was fit, heavily muscled and more than met the physical requirements. And he wasn't stupid. Now he knew Kenna wanted him, there was no way he'd let her walk away. Not now. Not ever.

She was *his*.

"You been a trader long, Steve?" The question came from Dex, and it took Xaan a moment to drag himself from pleasant thoughts of Kenna in a bonding gown, his jeweled collar at her throat.

"About twenty years or so," he replied, noting the guy was a little out of breath as they headed up the rise toward one of the towers. Add another reason why human males were inferior. Human females would be much better off with males of his kind.

"Career before then?" Dex wanted to know.

Before Xaan could answer, a sound in the undergrowth just ahead made all three humans whirl around skittishly.

The big Latharian warrior extended his senses, expanded and enhanced for battle when he was little more than a boy. A small mammal in the undergrowth had taken off as they approached—a prey species by its rapid departure. It was nothing to be worried about, but the humans with their limited senses didn't know that so he kept his face impassive. He felt sorry for them. To be so blind to their surroundings must be awful. Crippling. But they'd never known anything else. Was it better to never have had than to know and mourn the loss?

He turned back to Dex.

"Marine," he said, knowing they probably suspected some kind of military background from the way he moved. To deny it would just lay seeds of doubt in their minds, and he didn't want them looking at him any closer. Sure, he could walk and talk human, but he wasn't. Sooner or later, the cracks were going to show.

Dex grinned, fist-pumping the air. "I *knew* it. You owe me ten strips, Rob," he shot at the other man.

"We had a bet you were military of some kind. Rob here said you couldn't be, too young, but I just knew you were *something.* No one moves the way you do without some serious combat experience."

Oh, little human, you have no *idea,* Xaan thought, keeping his expression neutral.

"Come on then, spill. What were you? Recon? Armored?"

"Combat Engineer," Xaan replied, keeping as close to the truth as possible. Yes, his background was science, but Latharian science seemed to encompass areas humans considered engineering and, after decades as the emperor's champion, what he didn't know about combat wasn't worth knowing. It seemed to satisfy Dex, who nodded and returned his attention to the path as they walked.

Once again, he checked his communicator.

Perhaps the guy had a lover and he was waiting for a message? He was certainly waiting for something from someone.

It didn't take them long to leave the valley, their steps winding steadily upward. Their progress disturbed more of the wildlife, the humans around him getting more and more skittish with each rustle in the undergrowth. He shook his head to himself as the one on his left whirled around for the seventeenth time to check the bushes that side.

Finally they reached the booster tower on top of one of the highest hills that surrounded the valley. Xaan stopped, looking it up and down. Three times the height of the main colony building, it matched the three other towers he could see dotted around the edges of the valley. However, he could only see a third of the gleaming metalwork at the top. The rest of it was covered in thick vines. The base was a thick mass of green leaves and vicious looking thorns half the length of Xaan's forearm. Needle sharp, they evoked groans from Billy.

"Devil-plant," he muttered, reaching for a machete sheathed at his belt. "Fucking great. Fucking *hate* this stuff."

"Clear it out," Dex ordered, motioning them

both forward as he checked his communicator again. "We need to get to that control box."

The two men slung their rifles over their backs to start chopping into the thick plant life. Xaan watched impassively, arms folded over his broad chest. They hadn't asked him to help, and he hadn't brought his own weaponry. There was no way he was going near that plant without a laser cutter and heavy gauntlets. It seemed semi-sentient, the vines twisting and moving away, as though trying to escape the bite of the heavy machetes.

His decision was confirmed a few moments later. A vine, detached from its root by a heavy swing from Rob on the left, dropped. Its vicious thorns slashed across Billy's arm, whose back was turned for a moment as he dealt with a particularly stubborn tangle of vines. He grunted in pain as the lethally sharp thorns sliced through his skin. Blood splattered on the ground and across one of the lower vines.

It caused an instant reaction. Every thorn on the plant turned toward the blood, the soil beneath it writhing as though the roots themselves were also aware.

"Holy *shit!*" The two men stumbled back, trying to get away from the plants. Rob fell on his ass in his haste. He fumbled for his rifle, almost dropping it as he yanked it around.

"NO!" Dex and Xaan yelled at the same time, launching themselves forward to try and snatch the weapon from his hands, but it was too late. His finger jerked the trigger and held, the sharp retort of bullets ripping through the vines in a hail of devastation. The smell of sap filled the air as bits of vegetation splattered everywhere. Underneath it all, there was a metallic *ping-ping-ping* as the bullets tore through the radio repeater box. It exploded in a shower of sparks.

The bullets stopped, the rifle still clicking as the human kept his finger on the trigger with his gaze fixed on the now destroyed vines and radio like a rictus. His companion reached out and removed it from his grasp.

"Well fuck," Dex muttered, looking at the smoking remains of the radio. It was completely destroyed. "Looks like we got a long walk."

---

8

*T*he morning, although crisp at first, soon warmed up. Kenna closed her eyes as she walked with the other women, savoring the sweet breeze that swept through the valley toward them. It brought with it the scent of the heather-grasses that swept the edges of the valley. Obviously, it had dominated the valley before the colonists had cleared it for their crops.

She recognized some of them. High yield protein-wheats were used as the base for a lot of the mass-produced foods common through the Terran worlds. Most of it was bland and tasteless, but it was filling and provided adequate nutrition for the body, if not for the palate or soul. She knew the stuff well.

It was a staple of the marine corps' diet when deployed either in the field or on outer bases, but like recycled air, she hated it.

Some people were so poor, that all they had was money. Wall to wall luxuries and the best staterooms on orbital platforms with views of the rarest supernovas or spacial borealis. They breathed air filtered through ice-rock imported from the outer reaches and their water was infused with the rarest tri-platinum. And they thought they had it all.

They were wrong. This... the chance to walk through fields under the sun, her boots on real dirt and clean air in her lungs... these were real riches. And she intended to savor every moment.

The chatter of the women around her was the usual gossip—kids, teething... what romances were forming between who in the colony as kids whooped and ran about them. It was like a scene from her childhood before she'd gone into fleet service and for a while she just absorbed it.

Several of the women were armed, but she didn't think anything of it. Unless you were really lucky with a planet, there were always predators to be wary of. That was colony life.

"So... Suzie." One of the younger women at the

front of the group turned to smile over her shoulder. "How'd you meet that handsome hubby of yours?"

Kenna hid her small smile. Here it came, as she'd known it would. There wasn't a red-blooded woman alive who wouldn't be interested in Xaan. Just something about him, the way he moved, and the indefinable aura of danger that clung to him, even when he was relaxed and nonthreatening, hooked right into the primal part of a woman's reactions and sent her ovaries into overdrive. Must be something to do with the search for the strongest mate or something, she mused. So it made sense that women on a human colony would gravitate toward a Lathar man... a bigger, stronger and faster version of the human males they knew.

"Oh, it was the usual love story," she grinned. "Eyes meeting across a crowded room. Bar in the *Heleas Four* system... smoky, crowded, filled with merchants... then the place got shot to shit by mercenaries. Steve pulled me out of there after I got hit in the calf. Carried me to safety... It was so romantic." She sighed, playing the starry-eyed woman in love.

It actually wasn't too far from the truth, if you discounted the fact that Xaan had never carried her injured from a bar fight. She *had* been shot in the calf by mercs, though, on one of her first missions. She still had the starburst scar to prove it. And their eyes hadn't met for the first time over a smoke-filled, crowded bar. It had been a courtyard in the Imperial court, and he'd taken a gun off her after she'd threatened to ventilate a Latharian warrior's skull. To be fair, though, the warrior in question *had* been threatening her friend's now-husband. Kenna had taken exception to that and the asshole's assumption that any of the human women were his for the taking.

"Was it love at first sight?"

"Have you been together since?"

The questions came in thick and fast, making her smile broaden. Although she'd had female friends in the corps, and she'd been with a group of friends since the Lathar had taken them from the base, that group had dwindled a lot now as her friends had all paired off. She'd missed the simple chatter and concerns of colony women.

"Yes. It was love at first sight," she admitted, realizing it was true. "He was big and growly and I fell for him in a hot second. It just took me a while to get him to admit he felt the same."

"Men," a woman at the back chuckled. "Never see what's right under their damn noses."

"Ain't that the truth," Kenna replied as the soft laughter of the group surrounded her. Conversation continued until they reached the berry patches, as the group gently teased one of the younger women about a crush she had on one of the single men in the colony.

Splitting off into pairs, they worked through the scattered bushes, picking the ripe berries off the thorned stems. *Goojan* berries were sweet, kept well and made great preserves, but they couldn't be cultivated, so finding a patch like this must have been an unexpected but welcome bonus.

"Do you freeze these or make jam?" she asked Sami, the woman she was working with, and then popped another berry in her mouth. A small moan of pleasure escaped her as the tart, sweet taste exploded on her tongue. She'd already eaten more than she should, but the damn things were addictive.

"Both," Sami managed around a mouthful of berries. "And Maggie makes awesome pies as well. She might make one tonight if you're lucky."

"Oh." Disappointment filled Kenna at the news. *Goojan* berry pie was a rare treat. "I think Steve wanted to be gone by then. I'll have to see if I can persuade him to leave a little later. Here, grab this for me? I need to nip off for a moment..." She jerked her head toward the thicker bushes behind the berry patch and made a show of crossing her legs.

"Sure thing. Just make sure to use a stick and beat the longer grass," Sami warned, reaching out for Kenna's basket. "Some mean-ass snakes out this way and you don't want your lady garden to become snake-chow."

Kenna gave her the thumbs up as she walked away. Ducking into the thicker bushes, she turned right instead of left and skirted around the back quickly.

Breaking into a trot, she stayed just below the ridge line that ran around the edges of the fields. She didn't have long before she was missed, so she needed to make every second count. Not that she didn't trust the colony was exactly what it appeared to be—a fledging colony making its mark on its chosen planet—but she was a marine and nosey as hell. A sergeant early in her training had drummed it into her to trust but verify so something didn't bite her in the ass. Other than a snake, that was.

So she ran, legs eating up the distance quickly. She'd made sure to keep up her fitness levels during her time with the Lathar, which wasn't difficult in the warrior-based culture. She'd learned fighting techniques she'd never dreamed of and taught them a few tricks herself, especially the younger ones. Used to fighting larger opponents all her life, along with Dani Black—seriously, she was still fangirling over meeting the legendary general— she'd been able to show them how to level the playing field.

The fields looked normal and boring, so she discounted them. Nothing doing there. But the closer she got to the foothills, things got interesting. Voices ahead warned her to keep out of sight. Instinct and training made her keep to the ridgeline and low as she approached. Flat on her stomach, she moved forward to the top of the rise, using a clump of grass to keep herself hidden. Her top rode up, dirt and stones digging into the soft surface of her stomach, but she ignored the discomfort to peek between the long bushes.

"What the fuck?" she breathed as a frown furrowed her brow.

There was a junk yard hidden behind the rise, between the fields and the back of the colony buildings. But not just any junkyard. In a colony this size she'd have expected some broken down industrial machinery. Standard colony issue stuff was rugged, yes, and designed to work for many years without maintenance, but eventually they did need some care and attention.

This wasn't just industrial equipment though.

Her gaze widened as it wandered over machinery, small transports, even the skeleton of a ship bigger than Xaan's in the process of being stripped. But what made her breathing catch wasn't the ships, or the machines. It was the smashed-up ruins of a smaller colony and the large mound next to it. A chill went down her spine.

A destroyed colony and unmarked graves.

Xaan had been right. These people were lying to them.

She needed to warn him. And they needed to get off this planet. Fast.

Something was stalking them.

Halfway to the next tower Xaan's instincts went on high alert. Between one moment and the next, all the hackles rose on the back of his neck. Normally, he would have stilled instantly, snapping out a field command to alert those around him that there was a problem, but if he did that here... he could give away the fact he wasn't the human he was pretending to be.

So he continued walking, looking around circumspectly to check their surroundings. His fingers itched to go for the blaster normally holstered at his hip, but it wasn't there. No amount of playing human would matter if he'd come here openly carrying Latharian weaponry. The most he had was a small, non-descript knife in his boot so close in design to the ones he'd seen Kenna and her friend Jane use that it shouldn't cause comment. That was a weapon of last resort, though, one he didn't want the humans around him knowing about.

Nothing moved in the trees on either side of the ridge they walked along, the leaves and bushes suspiciously quiet. It was like all the animals nearby had registered the presence of a predator and had frozen. It wasn't because of the humans and, by extension, him... it couldn't be. They'd been hearing bird song all morning, proving the local wildlife was used to the colonists' activity out here.

No. This was something different. Something else had caused the silence. He could practically feel the tension in the air. The pent-up fear and adrenaline of the animals around them as they waited, ready to run for their lives if need be. Nature, on any planet, was dog-eat-dog, survival of the fittest, whether the dogs had four legs or eight.

Slowly, the humans around him started to become aware of the silence and the impending threat hanging like a malevolent cloud over them. They looked around, jumping at shadows as they belatedly made sure their weapons were all close at hand.

Lady goddess above. Xaan had to stop himself shaking his head. They were bloody clueless. How the *draanth* had they survived this long without either being wiped out or wiping themselves out? If whatever it was hidden in the shadows had been an *Ovverta* or even a *Krin,* they'd have been fucked even before they realized they were fucked.

A cold chill rolled down his spine at the thought. *Could* it be a *Krin*? There was no way it was an *Ovverta.* They were near extinct, with no more than a handful of breeding pairs left. Little more than a footnote in the history of the universe.

But the *Krin*? The predatory, carnivorous race was very much alive and well. Unfortunately. Many races would breathe a sigh of relief if they were as extinct as the *Ovverta.* But they weren't. They still hunted their territory in the outer reaches of the galaxy, an area cordoned off with big warnings left there by every other sentient race that to cross the line was a death sentence.

They'd have left it at that, but the eight-armed bastards didn't like staying in their territory. Oh no, they preferred prey from the inner systems. Intelligent, sentient prey that screamed as it was being devoured alive.

But not all inner system species were hunted. Although the Lathar were considered a rare delicacy by the *Krin*, they'd long ago learned that the Lathar not only fought back, but that any incursion against them caused a violent reaction beyond anything they could cope with, often resulting in them losing multiple breeding pods in retaliation for each Latharian victim.

No, it couldn't be a *Krin*, Xaan told himself. If it was, the colonists would already be dead, or in the larder of the *Krin's* ship. There was no way it would have let any of them escape. Not when it had found a planet without defenses. It would be like all its *draanthic* pod-days had come at once, and it had landed in the middle of an all-you-can-eat buffet.

Plus, the wounds on those two bodies were telling. Krin did not mangle their food like that. Or leave so many juicy bits to rot and decay. They might leave the husk of a corpse, discarded like some empty nutrition wrapper, but that hadn't been the case with the bodies in the colony medical bay.

Yes, some of the torso had been excised, but the chest and abdominal cavities had been largely intact. Which wasn't indicative of a *Krin* attack. No *Krin* would have been able to resist the lure of a live, beating heart and a pair of breathing lungs. He'd seen them himself, in the inner systems, practically salivating as other species walked by them. Only the control collars they were forced to wear in polite society and the threat of Latharian or even Krynassis retaliation kept their murderous impulses in check.

"Keep it sharp," Dex murmured. "Predators in this area," he added as an aside to Xaan, as though to explain why normally macho males were jumping at shadows suddenly.

Xaan frowned. "Why did you pick this planet if the wildlife is so hostile?"

He might not have been a colonist—the planets he'd always made his home on had been Latharian for countless generations—but he knew there were lots of tests and surveys before resources were committed to placing a colony on any planet. At least, that's how it worked with his people's colonies. He couldn't see human ones working much differently. It would be illogical to commit lives and resources to a planet where there was a high probability of the colonists dying or being killed by creatures unknown.

"Didn't get much choice," Billy grumbled bitterly. A hard look from Dex shut him up fast, and he fiddled with his rifle, the dressing on his arm making his movements clumsy.

"The planners decided on the planet, not us," Dex explained smoothly. "Turns out the predators hibernate. There was no evidence of them when they did the surveys."

Xaan's lips compressed into a line. That seemed reasonable. Terran technology was much less advanced. It was entirely possible they couldn't track death rates and causes in the local animal remains. Frustration surged through him again as his joking words to Kenna came back to haunt him. Humans really *were* space toddlers who shouldn't have been allowed out of their own solar system.

It didn't take them long, walking in silence, to reach the next tower. Unlike the first, this one was clear of bloodthirsty vines. But, unlike the first tower, the beacon housing was bent and buckled like something hard had hit it repeatedly. One hinge was broken, and the door was twisted in the frame. He frowned.

It looked like the damn thing was stuck in there. Approaching, he ran his fingertips around the edges of the door, testing to see if there was even the slightest bit he could get a grip on. But no, there wasn't even a hairsbreadth lip he could grab onto.

Stepping back, he studied the door, shaking his head. "Nope, that dr—bastard is totally jammed in there," he said, quickly correcting himself.

"Do you need a lever or something to open it up?" Dex's voice was distracted and he was looking at his communication device again. Xaan shook his head, looking back at the door again, frowning.

"Hmmm, nope. I think I got it."

Stepping up to the casing again, he slammed his booted foot into the door. It impacted heavily with the bottom corner and the door popped free with a metallic screech of complaint.

"Woah!" Rob whistled. "Lad's got some skills."

"Percussive maintenance," Xaan chuckled as he knelt down to open the casing fully and look inside. He was so focused on looking for a problem that he didn't notice at first that the beacon was fully operational. It was only when he couldn't immediately spot the fault that he realized. And frowned. What the *draanth*?

Sitting back on his heels, he was about to ask

Dex how the beacon relays were set up, but his words were cut off as something hard and metallic pressed against the back of his skull.

He froze. The feel of a muzzle was unmistakable, no matter what species technology it belonged to. Without moving, he opened up all his senses. He knew it was Dex directly behind him, a gun pressed up against his skull. He could smell the tang of the male's sweat and his cologne, different from the nothing the other two males wore.

He also knew Dex was too close. And that was because they didn't have any clue who or *what* Xaan was. They thought he was Steve Renner, an ex-marine, outer systems trader on the edge of his luck. They had no clue what he really was. If they did, they'd have been running the other way. They certainly wouldn't have set up this little scenario.

Anyone who knew anything about the Lathar and its warriors knew you didn't get within range like this. It would take less than a heartbeat for Xaan to twist, yank the gun out of Dex's hands and put a bullet through his brain.

The problem was the other two. Just because Billy and Rob were human didn't mean he'd discounted them as a threat. He'd seen how they handled the rifles they carried. And even panicked,

Billy had a damn good aim. He couldn't be sure they weren't good enough to nail him as soon as he moved a muscle.

Before he could formulate a plan, though, Dex's next words ensured he wouldn't fight back. "Play nice, or your pretty little wife will die."

9

*K*enna had made it back to the group, and to her berry picking partner, without incident. She'd even managed to explain away her extended absence with a grimace and a muttered comment about the good food "going right through her." Since it was a common occurrence when going to real food from space rations, Sami just sympathized and handed her basket back so they could continue picking berries. But the scales were off Kenna's eyes now. Even if she didn't betray it by so much as a glance or a change in expression, she was hyperaware of everything and everyone around her.

Who were these people? The fact they weren't the original colonists, at least not all of them, was obvious. She'd bet her life that the original colonists were buried in that mass grave. And those ruined buildings. That was a colony with at least a few years' growth. More than enough to explain the discrepancy in time and the extra chiller cabinets in the hospital bay. She'd been wondering about that since yesterday.

Tech was expensive, so colonies were often on a budget when it came to the fancy toys. Most things were sent with component parts and matter printers so the colonists could print out what they required to build whatever item they needed. They saved space and weight that way. But certain items, like medical equipment, were delicate and needed to be specially built to specific tolerances, so they were sent prebuilt. Like chiller cabinets. But each colony usually only had four, not eight. Eight was a lot for one colony. Too many. She'd been explaining it away by the possibility this was a medical research colony... but there weren't enough doctors.

No, she mused, as the group trudged back to the colony with full baskets. A scavenger colony made much more sense. Especially now she'd seen the remains of the previous one. They weren't common, operating solely on the outer edges of human space. No one was sure how they'd started. Perhaps two colonies in the same system, one failing, which then decided to take over its neighbor.

However they'd started, rumor ran rife in the colony community about them. How they descended from the skies, razing the colony buildings to the ground and killing people before taking over. They usually killed the men and children, just leaving alive fertile women to breed with. And not in the way the Lathar took women to breed with either. Those captured by scavengers were little more than sex slaves.

She needed to tell Xaan, and they needed to get the hell off this planet. Her expression was set, jaw working as the settlement came into view. As soon as they reached comms range, she needed to let the authorities know. Scavenger colonies were the lowest of the low. They needed fucking over as badly as they fucked their victims over. She'd settle for them being thrown in Mirax Ruas.

They reached the edge of the compound, walking along the fortified walls toward the main gate with their boots kicking up dust as they went. The fortifications made more sense now. She doubted it was anything to do with native predators, and far more to do with the fact that they were worried about someone attacking them. There was more than one scavenger group out there and this world was a peach of a prize.

The gates opened for them, not fully but just enough to let them through single file. The group dutifully filed through the narrow gap between the heavy metal sheets. As soon as Kenna stepped through, all her senses went on alert. Two men, armed with rifles, cut off her escape from behind and Dex walked toward her, his face set in grim lines.

"Sorry, gotta go," Sami muttered, grabbing Kenna's basket and making a break for it. Kenna didn't argue. The situation had obviously gone to hell in a heartbeat, so she needed both hands free. A basket full of fruit wasn't an optimal weapon.

"W-what's going on?"

She played up her confusion in a breathy voice, looking from the two men behind her to Dex with wide eyes. Let them lap up the act of the surprised and less-capable-than-them female trader. Traders weren't usually aggressive. Accustomed to pirates, they often gave over their cargo without a fight, preferring to keep their ships and their necks intact for another day.

"Come with me please, Mrs. Renner," Dex said, his voice low and measured, the deep tones serious.

"I'm afraid there's been an incident with your husband."

"Oh my god," she reached Dex's side, her expression painted with concern, some of it real. "Is he okay? Did he get hurt?"

Dex slid her a sideways glance, his pale eyes guarded. "A little yes, but it was self-defense..."

"Self-defense? What do you mean?" She frowned as he hurried them along. They skirted the outside of the main settlement—she couldn't even bring herself to call it a colony anymore—buildings. There was another group set behind them. From the age and design, as well as the placements, these must have been garages or workshops from the original colony. The matter printing was different, obviously done on an older machine than the rest of the colony. So that was at least two colonies they'd scavenged from.

Dex stopped her before they entered the largest building, his expression one of concern as he reached out to touch her upper arm in reassurance. "I'm sorry to tell you, but... he attacked one of our workers. Nearly killed him. Rob had to drag him off."

She managed to hide her raised eyebrow behind a stunned expression. She heard his words, but she just couldn't make them jive in her brain. There were two problems with what he said. One, Xaan would not have broken cover and just attacked someone... and two, if he had, there would have been no way a human could have pulled him off, injuring him in the process.

She'd seen Xaan fight. Even healing from the horrendous injuries he'd received in his last battle, he was still the most lethal thing she'd ever seen on two legs. There was no way any human could beat him. Which meant one thing. He'd let them beat him.

"Oh my god," she managed, covering her mouth with her hand. She even managed a small tremble of her hand and a wobble in her voice. She needed to be on the stage for that one.

Dex's expression softened a little and he reached out to touch her arm reassuringly. "He's not badly hurt, but..."

His expression twisted a little. "How long have you known him? I'm sorry, but I think he might be a spy for them Latharians."

He was so near to the truth Kenna nearly laughed right in his face.

"*What?*"

Dex nodded, obviously taking her gasped

exclamation to be shock. "I'm sorry, my dear, but it's the only explanation. He damaged the radio beacon rather than helping us mend it and attacked Billy when he spotted it. Them Latharians... they'd kill to get this planet. And our women. Sexual deviants, they are. Need women for their breeding programs. Got 'em lined up in wards, being fucked over and over by different alien men until they get pregnant."

She blinked, shaking her head. If only they knew. The Lathar didn't need to steal any Terran planets, much less one scratty little planet in the ass-end of beyond. And *breeding programs?* That idea was so ludicrous she couldn't even muster a laugh. If this guy thought any Latharian male would allow another anywhere near his female after he'd claimed her... that the Lathar as a whole would disrespect women like that... Was this the shit about the Lathar that was being pedaled as truth within the Terran systems?

"Oh my god." Back with the breathy voice, she added a little step toward Dex, casting a look about her as though she expected Latharian warriors to jump out of the shadows and kidnap her away to put her in one of these breeding programs. "You think so?"

"Uh-huh, yes." Dex nodded, not clever enough to

hide the pleasure in his eyes that she seemed to be buying into his fairytale. "Now brace yourself, my dear. I need you to talk to him. We need access to his ship systems so we can look at his coordinate and comms logs. See how much contact he's had with them so we can pass it along to the authorities. Unless *you* know the codes to unlock the ship?"

So that's what they were after. Even though Xaan's ship appeared to be a Terran trader, it had component parts they could use. Instantly she knew that her and Xaan's future contained an unmarked grave somewhere out in the wilds behind the new settlement.

"No," she shook her head, her eyes still wide. "He never lets me have them. We've only been married a few years. I-I don't know what he did before that."

Dex's eyes narrowed. "I thought he was a marine. Combat engineers?"

That was what he'd told them? A sudden image of Xaan in marine uniform made her suck in a breath, but the image quickly reverted back to him in his combat leathers. She shook her head slowly.

"I don't think so? I think he grew up in the Aarborian Borealis?" she added, naming a famously pacifist sector of space. The worlds there didn't believe in violence against others. Personally she thought they were tree-hugging idealists, but to each their own.

Dex's grin was as swift as it was quickly concealed. Triumph flared in his eyes. "I knew there was something off with his story. Are you ready, my dear?"

She nodded, allowing the settlement leader to herd her through the door into the shadowed interior of the building. The light touch of his hand on her lower back made her freeze up a little. She'd grown so unaccustomed to male contact, so used to the formalities and customs of the Latharian court, that to be touched without her permission by a male she wasn't intimate with almost had her spinning around and introducing Dex's nose to the wall. Several times.

Keeping the impulse in check, she walked with him down a short corridor and into a room. A quick scan confirmed they were in what had once been a garage and machine workshop. However, the interior had been stripped and cleared. Instead of the benches, cranes and jacks she'd have expected in here, there were cells. Honest to god cells. Two down either side of the room. The two opposite were occupied.

Her gaze narrowed. Xaan was in one, sitting

down, leaning against the back wall while the other held a human man lying on a rough pallet who looked like he'd been well and truly worked over. Some kind of bot was in the cell with him, in a heap like a puppet with its strings cut.

Her gaze immediately cut back to Xaan. He met her eyes levelly, the tiny movement of his hand giving her all the information she needed. During her time with the Lathar, he'd taught her their field signals.

Hostile. Cover your ass. Stay free.

She covered her mouth with a gasp, the small downward sweep of her eyelids telling him his message was received and understood.

"And you think he's a spy?" she asked Dex in a whisper, taking a little half step toward the human. He made her skin crawl but she had to maintain her cover.

"I'm afraid so, my dear," Dex replied, putting an arm around her waist to comfort her.

The sudden glitter of Xaan's eyes told her the instant he got free, Dex was a dead man. Violently dead. She couldn't find it in her to be sorry about that. Not if this guy was a scavenger. Leaning into him with a sigh, she let a tear roll down her cheek.

"I think I might be able to work out the codes,"

she whispered. "Given a little time. Will you keep him in here? What about the other one?"

"Yes," Dex nodded, starting to draw her from the room. "The other one is a spy too. Found him in an escape pod with alien tech. They'll be tried by a jury of the people for their crimes and executed."

She let loose a sob, concealing her laughter as cries of sorrow and let him take her back to the main buildings. She didn't know yet how she was going to get Xaan and the other man free, but she knew one thing...

These scavenger assholes were going to rue the day they'd been born.

Pride filled Xaan. Kenna had gotten the message within the blink of an eye. His little female was as smart as she was resourceful. He wasn't fooled for a moment by her helpless act as she clung to Dex, but the human male lapped it up, shooting a smile of triumph over Kenna's head as he wrapped an arm around her and led her from the building. It was a look that gloated. A look that said he'd taken everything of Xaan's—his freedom, his ship and now his woman.

It was all Xaan could do not to chortle in

amusement. No wonder all the human females he'd met so far preferred Latharian males if this was the best their own species had to offer. His hard gaze tracked Dex until they were through the door and out of the building, noting the hand across the back of Kenna's waist. Dex would pay for that one. Xaan would remove his hand, at the neck, for touching Xaan's woman.

He had noticed the slight stiffening of Kenna's frame as the male touched her. She was obviously uncomfortable, even if she hid it well, and pleasure filled Xaan's chest at the small proof his woman disliked being touched by others. That was how it should be. She was *his*. And as soon as he was out of this damn cell, he'd claim her in every sense of the word, leaving her in absolutely no doubt of that fact.

He closed his eyes and leaned against the wall of the cell as the outer door slammed shut. A mass of bruises and cuts, his body ached all over. The three men had worked him over with something akin to glee, demanding the codes to his ship, before dragging him back to throw him in here when he wouldn't give them to them.

Concerned for Kenna's safety, he hadn't fought back, but his instinct had been right about Dex not wanting to kill Kenna as he'd threatened. No, the human male was too interested in bedding her for that. As expected, he'd tried to turn her against Xaan to get what he wanted.

Idiot human thought he was a player. He had no clue he was being played himself.

Xaan snorted and stretched as he assessed the condition of his body. The cuts and bruises weren't too bad. While they might have put a human down for a while... He wasn't human. He was Lathar. He'd had worse, much worse, and that was just in the course of training. He was fully battle ready and more than these assholes could handle.

They'd definitely messed with the wrong male.

Especially as, even through their ham-handed interrogation and beating, they'd totally forgotten to search him. The knife was still safely concealed in his boot. He grinned, unable to stop the small sound of amusement escaping his lips. Really, this was like child's play. Perhaps he should set something up like this as a training exercise for the young warriors? It was certainly a new situation—one they wouldn't have experienced before.

The sound appeared to disturb the occupant of the cell next to Xaan's. A human male lay on his side, in a much worse state than Xaan himself. He looked like he'd been pulled from a battlefield or an accident of some kind. His uniform was tattered and burned in places, blood-stained in others. He seemed to have a collection of injuries, the newer ones Xaan suspected had been inflicted by Dex and his friends.

What interested Xaan though, was the uniform. It was similar to the ones he'd seem Kenna and her friend Jane wear in images he'd seen in their terran files. This man... Xaan tilted his head to read the name on the breast pocket. Stephens... This man, Stephens, was Terran military. A marine like Kenna.

"Hey there," he said as the man's eyes opened slowly. At least, the left one did. The right was nearly swollen shut. "Back in the land of the living?"

Stephens swallowed and groaned as he rolled painfully to a sitting position against the wall. He looked over at Xaan, the swift assessing look telling the Latharian warrior there was nothing wrong with the human's mind or instincts.

"They get you as well?" Stephens asked, his voice almost as deep as Xaan's. "Bad luck, dude."

Xaan gave a small grunt of confirmation. "Fell for the distress call trick. You?"

As soon as he'd felt that muzzle at the back of his head, just above the juncture between skull and spine, he'd figured it out. The colony broadcast a distress call to bring in its prey. Then once it was in the web, they pounced like a spider to feast. It was a neat trick that got them new technology and replacement parts, as well as new blood, if they were lucky.

"Nah." Stephens shook his head. "I was the one in distress. My ship was attacked and destroyed. Ended up in an escape pod somehow." He rubbed the back of his neck, a frown creasing his brow. "Then crashed here. They picked me up after I ejected from the pod. Don't recall that part. The pod was destroyed before they got to me."

The man's voice was level but Xaan easily picked up the confusion as he couldn't recall part of the chain of events. That wasn't a surprise. If his ship had been destroyed and then he'd ejected from an escape pod... human bodies were more fragile than Latharian ones, and the angry bruising at his temple told Xaan the male had taken at least one knock to the head. Memory loss was to be expected.

But... Xaan's gaze slid sideways to the crumpled form of a bot in the corner of the cell. "That with you in the pod?"

Stephens held Xaan's gaze with his good eye. "Yes. It's a new experimental unit. They want me to wake it up since it apparently destroyed the pod while I was out of it. But its battery is dead."

Xaan nodded at the male's explanation but he knew it was utter *trallshit*. The unit wasn't new or experimental. It was a regular Latharian worker bot, the kind used for maintenance aboard most ships. They ran on automated routines and did the dirty jobs to free up warriors stationed aboard for other duties. But... they were hardcoded to protect life. It would be more than capable of getting an incapacitated warrior, or a being it had registered as Latharian, off a damaged ship and into an escape pod.

What was interesting though was that it had removed Stephens from the pod and destroyed it. Why would it bother? He'd studied the schematics from human ships, and like Latharian ones, the pods were designed for one way trips. The thing wouldn't fly again, so why destroy it? Random destruction wasn't coded into their neural nets.

"Your ship was experimental?" Xaan asked with interest, studying the bot. It wasn't a combat model, so there was no onboard weaponry, but that didn't mean it was harmless. Worker bots were built on the same chassis as combat ones, the limiting factor was the workers were operated by non-AI computer "brains."

Even though Latharian ships were often fitted with AIs, laws had been passed years ago that banned their use in avatar bodies. An AI had been fitted into a physical body in an attempt to create invulnerable troops for the battlefield. The thing, previously stable, had gone mad and killed dozens before it was finally put down, and laws had been passed the same day. Now, if an AI was found to have downloaded into anything approaching a Latharian form, it was instantly destroyed. No one wanted a repeat of the same tragedy.

"Yes," Stephens replied but Xaan could tell he was lying. Oh, he was good at it. He didn't display the normal body language clues that gave away the falsehood. Instead, he was still, his gaze intent and focused on Xaan. Too focused. Like he was trying to will Xaan to believe him. The tiny change in his breathing combined with Xaan's gut instinct... all added up to indicate the human was lying.

"Huh. Nice gig if you can get it." Xaan shrugged.

He settled himself back more comfortably against the wall and looked around their prison. Stephens was hiding the fact that the bot was alien tech, but did that mean he couldn't trust the male?

He could do with an ally on the inside as well as the outside. And if that bot had an active database and uplink, he might be able to access the beacons and use them to boost the signal to call for help. It was a long shot, but it was better than nothing.

Even better if he could get the bot working. A few command codes and he could set it to register only him, Kenna and Stephens as Latharian. Any move Dex and his little friends made then would be met with extreme violence. Between him and the bot? They were fucked, well and truly.

He studied Stephens out the corner of his eye. So far he hadn't been impressed by human males. Dex, the few he'd seen here...the ones he'd dealt with in Terran high command who had consistently tried to screw the Lathar over. None of them had inspired confidence.

But there was something about the way Stephens held himself, the air of capability around him and the look in his eye. If Xaan didn't know better, he could have sworn the male was Lathar. He was even built along the same lines, if a little smaller. He had similar muscle mass, but not the height. Perhaps some Latharian traits *had* survived in the males?

He made a snap judgement, looking directly at Stephens.

"You are aware it's Latharian?"

Stephens didn't react, not by so much as a flicker of his eyelid.

"Now why would you go and say a thing like that?" he asked. "You don't strike me as the same sort of paranoid fuck Dex is, seeing aliens around every corner."

Xaan's lips quirked. Oh yes, this one was as sharp as a combat dagger. "I'm not paranoid, no. You're asking the wrong question though."

"Oh?" Stephens' eyebrow winged up for a second. "What question should I be asking?"

Xaan let the silence stretch out for long seconds. "You should be asking why I recognize that it's Latharian technology. Specifically worker model HC-seven-four-nine... Probably B class."

Stephens' eyes narrowed a little. Just a fraction in the corners. "That level of knowledge?" His gaze flicked over Xaan in much the same way Xaan had just assessed him. "The muscle you're packing and the fact you're hiding both that you're not that injured and behind that frankly terrible trader accent? I'd say you were Latharian yourself."

Xaan allowed the slow grin to spread over his face. "Perhaps human males aren't so dumb after all."

Stephens' eyes widened in shock, quickly controlled. "Shit. You are? That was a wild guess."

Xaan inclined his head. "I am. You're more perceptive than most."

"Who are you?" Stephens fired the question, back on mission almost immediately, a fact that pleased Xaan. Yeah, he'd written human males off prematurely.

"It doesn't matter who I am, just that I'm here. Which massively increases your chances of survival. If you're with me?"

10

"*I*'m so sorry that you had to find out this way, my dear. It must be an awful shock," Dex said, his face a mask of false concern and understanding as he sat opposite her in the canteen area of the main building.

Kenna kept her fantasies of killing him with the tin coffee mug in her hand to herself and shrugged. "Love is blind sometimes," she murmured softly, keeping an upset little catch in her voice. So far they were buying the shocked wife routine.

"Thank you," she murmured to Maggie as the older woman put down a plate of flatcakes with some of the berries they'd picked this morning on the side.

"We had a whirlwind courtship and married

within a week," she revealed, reaching out for a cake. She was supposed to be upset, but food was food and as a marine she'd long ago learned to eat and sleep whenever she could. "Sorry," she mumbled around a mouthful of cake. "Comfort eater."

"You eat as many as you like, love," Maggie said with a smile, squeezing her shoulder before moving off to yell at someone in the back of the kitchen area, "*No, don't put that down there! Bloody hell, have to do everything myself!*"

Dex smiled as the big woman bustled off. "Bloody miracle, she is. No idea what I'd do without her."

Kenna gave a small smile, her gaze following Maggie for a moment. She looked like everyone's favorite grandma, but she was obviously one of Dex's most trusted people. What colony had she come from and why had she joined the scavengers? How many people had she helped to kill? How many in that mass grave were down to her? It went to show that appearances could be deceptive. Just because someone looked like butter wouldn't melt in their mouth didn't mean they were good. The most innocent and pure appearance could conceal the blackest of hearts.

Like her, for example. Here she was pretending

to be a heartbroken bride when in reality she was plotting how quickly she could get these people in a cell for their crimes. And, she realized, if she couldn't put them in a cell, she'd happily put them into the same mass grave they'd condemned so many of their victims to. Because she doubted this was the first colony they'd taken over.

"So... how are you feeling?" Dex drew her attention back to him with a soft comment and a gentle touch on her arm. He really was pulling out all the stops with her. Classic understanding shoulder to cry on. She knew the next part of his play... A shoulder to cry on became a dick to ride on. That's what they said, wasn't it? Some point soon, Dex was going to make his interest in her known. For "when she was ready" of course, but he'd let her know she was welcome to join them at his side, and in his bed.

"I'll get there." She offered him a small, tremulous smile. "I just can't believe it, you know? A spy? For *them?* The aliens?" She looked around as though the Lathar would overhear them and leap out of the shadows.

"I mean... where did he meet them? How did they get to him? He's *human* for heaven's sakes! What would persuade him to betray his own people?" she cried, laying it on thick. They obviously didn't suspect Xaan wasn't human and she didn't want them to start thinking down that route. He could end up like one of the bodies in the mortuary cabinets.

A cold chill rolled down her spine. Had Dex done that to those poor people? She didn't believe him as far as she could throw him about how they'd died. No predator caused injuries like that. It looked more like they'd been in heavy combat or an industrial accident. Perhaps that was it. They'd died in the battle when the colony had been taken over, and Dex and his lot had mutilated the bodies to show poor saps who turned up, lured in by their fake distress signal like her and Xaan.

"I don't know, my dear. There, there... it's all going to be alright," he murmured, shifting around to the chair next to her to pull her into a reassuring embrace against one bony shoulder. While he was almost as tall as Xaan, he didn't have anywhere near the same muscle mass. Her skin crawled as he patted her back, as though it were trying to escape his touch. She managed to stop herself flinching and remained still.

A prickle across the back of her neck made her open her eyes and she spotted a woman near the kitchen glaring at her. It was Bulldog again, the same woman who'd stopped the young girl from talking to Kenna last night.

Unlike Maggie, who was all smiles and grandmotherly concern, Bulldog's look made no pretense about the fact she didn't like Kenna. Not one little bit. That one she *could* believe had dumped people into a mass grave. Her gaze flickered toward Dex and her hostility made sense. She was interested in the scavenger leader.

You're welcome to him, sweetheart, Kenna thought as she managed to extricate herself from Dex's octopus-like hands.

"T-Thank you." She wiped at her eyes with the back of her hand. Where she'd managed to drag up some tears from she had no idea, but she had. Perhaps she should look into a new career in acting when she got back to Lathar Prime... "Most people would have lumped me in that cell with him. Assumed I was a traitor as well."

"I would never think of you that way, my dear. It can't have escaped your notice that I think a lot of you..." Dex reached out to cover her hands with one of his, his expression serious but soft. *Here it came.* "Obviously it's way too early to think of things like that, but I'd just like you to know that there will always be a place for you here. With me..."

She schooled her expression. She *knew* the asshole would try and make a move on her at some point.

Carefully, she framed a teary, but surprised expression. "I'm... err, really? I-I'm flattered," she looked away, but even as good as her acting skills were, she couldn't pull a blush out of the hat. Pale and interesting would have to do.

She snuck a glance up at him from under her lashes, feeling sick as she played the flustered but flattered... what... spy's estranged wife? "I'm... I couldn't yet. Not with it being so soon after..." She trailed off and looked away.

"Yes... yes. When you're ready, of course, my dear," he said benevolently, patting her hand. "I just wanted you to know so you didn't worry. Your future is assured."

That last line made her pause, and in an instant she realized that had she been what she appeared, the wife of a trader falsely accused by Dex, her fate was already sealed. "Steve" would no doubt have met with an accident, leaving Dex clear to move in on the young widow.

She had to get Xaan out of there, and fast.

Because trying to kill a Latharian warrior of Xaan's level was only going to end one way—brutal and bloody violence that would blow their cover six ways to Sunday.

"Thank you so much." She looked down at the data console on the table in front of them. It was an older model, a type often used by the colonies because it was rugged and reliable. She dragged it toward her. "Let me work on breaking his codes so we can open up the ship. I want to know how much he's screwed humanity over... and he has my shit still on his ship. I want it back."

THEY WERE WATCHING HER.

Kenna kept up her pretense of a betrayed wife all through the afternoon and evening meal. It didn't take much. They were all so ready to believe "Steve" was a spy. She'd caught hints of the conversation through dinner. Whispers as they all looked her way with pity—stereotyping him because he was "too good-looking" and "they'd known something was up." Comments about that "poor young woman all alone now" had made her blink. Either they were all expert actors trying to mess with her head, or at least some of them had bought into Dex's bullshit.

She sighed into the darkness as she sat on the compound wall looking out. She'd come out here after dinner, murmuring to the guards that she needed to clear her head. A nod and she'd been waved through but, for the last hour, they'd watched her carefully.

So they should. Her only reason for coming up here was to see where she could drop down the wall on the other side and make it to the ship. She was pretty sure Xaan would have set the security system so she could access it, and she'd like to see the walls of that prison stand up against Latharian shipboard weapons. She'd blow the *shit* out of the place to get him out.

But she couldn't do any of that while the freaking guards were watching her like hawks. She felt like she was under the damn microscope. *Get bored. Wander off,* she mentally urged them. *Nothing to see here.* She managed to stop just short of waving at them. She wasn't supposed to be as perceptive as that.

Just when she thought she might be able to slip away into the shadows, footsteps behind her made her turn around. Inwardly, she suppressed a sigh. Dex was coming along the catwalk at the top of the wall toward her, his expression splitting into a smile as he saw her looking.

But he was just a fraction of a second too late. She'd seen the cold and calculating look he'd covered up quickly. Yeah... if she really was Suzie Renner and she turned him down, she'd end up in the same unmarked grave as her husband. Dex wasn't the type to take no for an answer.

"Hey," she smiled as he got closer. "Couldn't sleep either? I came up here to clear my head." She motioned to the valley around them, the fields painted in shades of grey and midnight, silver glimmers from the triad moons above casting highlights over the top of the crops and drawing the line of the river to the west. "This view, huh? I can totes see why you guys decided on this place."

Dex took a seat on the block next to her, obviously dragged up here on purpose. "Yeah..." He looked out over the valley. "It's paradise alright. We count ourselves lucky every day."

Huh. Paradise rotten more like.

Kenna kept her thoughts to herself as she slid a sideways glance at the guy. She had to give something, she knew that, to keep them off the scent. So far she'd piddled about all day pretending to try and break Xaan's encryption codes on his ship when in reality she'd just been moving numbers around.

"I *could* see myself settling down here," she admitted in a soft voice. "It's so beautiful."

Dex reached out to pat her knee, his voice filled with pleasure. "You have no idea how much that means to me. Obviously, this is all on your terms... when *you're* ready. Not before. I promise."

Yeah, like she'd trust the word of a murdering, psycho scavenger. But she nodded and smiled, sliding him another coy little glance from under her lashes.

"Well," she said, a little too brightly. "I should get some sleep. Get an early start on that code tomorrow so we can get into the ship. Perhaps we can even use the radio to mend the one here?" she added with a smile. "And we have other stuff on board that I'm sure will make life a little easier here."

"Of course, my dear. You get some rest." Dex reached out and captured her hand before she could move away, bringing it to his lips to kiss the back of her knuckles. It was all she could do not to yank it from his grasp and land a solid right hook in his jaw. "Sleep well."

"Thank you," she murmured, pulling her hand back. "You too."

Walking away quickly across the catwalk to the nearest down ladder, she quickly readjusted her plans. There was no sense in trying to get over the wall tonight, not after the conversation with Dex. She doubted he'd come up there just to chat her up. No, he'd been checking she wasn't doing exactly what she was about to and make a break for it.

Plan b, she decided, climbing down the ladder with practiced ease. It wasn't something that would give her away. As a trader, she'd have been up and down ladders into and out of cargo holds all the time.

Her booted feet hit the ground and she walked off toward the building her room was in, rubbing at the back of her neck tiredly. But as soon as she reached the first set of shadows, she slid to the right and circled back around the main building instead. Keeping hidden, she moved fast, heading toward the workshops Xaan was being held in. She needed to let him know what she'd learned... that these assholes weren't innocent colonists but career murderers.

Her breathing rasped in her ears as she kept to the shadows and started to work her way across the compound. Halfway around, she paused suddenly, a sound in the shadows behind her making her freeze.

Going down on one knee, she listened, trying to catch every little bit of sound. It had sounded like someone creeping up behind her.

Shit. Her heart sped up a little. She couldn't afford to get caught out here, not this late. While Dex was still chatting her up as a potential bedmate, she had a little wriggle room with certain things, but this... he'd know instantly that Suzie Renner wasn't on the level and she'd end up in the cell next to Xaan's. Or in a chiller cabinet as a grisly warning to the next people to fall prey to the distress call con.

She stayed still so long she started to chill, a shiver running down her spine. The heat of the day had long disappeared and the temperature had dropped sharply. She wouldn't want to spend long out in the open. That was for sure. There were no other sounds behind her. No shouts of alarm and clattering of feet. The spotlights mounted on the compound wall didn't turn and stab through the darkness to pick her out.

Okay... she was just hearing things then. Good. That was better than the alternative.

Shaking herself, she moved again, slower this time. She'd only made it half the rest of the distance to the prison when the sound of an altercation nearby caught her attention. There was a muffled, feminine squeak, and the sound of cloth being ripped... the meaty sound of a hand hitting flesh.

"Get yourself in there and shut the fuck up, you stupid little bitch," a man hissed, his voice low and full of threat. *"You don't want to be useless. Do you? You know what happens to useless people around here... Remember your parents, don'tcha? Wanna end up like that?"*

Kenna flattened herself to the wall and crept toward the corner, nearer the voice. She peeked around to see the teenager she'd tried to talk to in the restroom being dragged by one of Dex's men toward a small building set apart from the main group.

The girl looked terrified, her face pale in the darkness as the man shoved her through the door. It took everything Kenna had to stay concealed in the shadows, fury raging through every cell in her body. The guy's words confirmed what she already knew. These assholes were scavengers who had killed most of the original colonists. Obviously the girl, who looked to be in her late teens, had caught the eye of one of them and she'd been spared.

Mulling that over, Kenna turned and melted into the shadows again. It tore at her to leave the girl in that asshole's clutches, but she couldn't do anything to help anyone if she was in a cell alongside Xaan. She needed to get them free first, and then by all that was holy, she would come back for the girl.

Less than a minute later, though, she ran into trouble. The settlement was laid out haphazardly, with no rhyme or reason she could see. So there were gaps between buildings and the shadows she was using to conceal herself. Gaps that were brightly lit by the moons overhead. She glared up at the sky. And the bastards were plural, so when one went behind a cloud the others were shining merrily, leaving her no window of opportunity.

She stopped at the edge of one set of shadows, looking across at the building opposite. There was no other way around—not without going all the way around the compound—and the longer she was out here, the greater the chance she'd be caught. But that was a at least twenty feet without any kind of cover. Which meant if she stepped out of the shadows and someone walked around the corner, they'd spot her like a rabbit in the headlights.

"Do you think she'll do it?" A deep voice warned her a second before Dex and another man walked around the corner.

Kenna froze in place, measuring her breathing. She was still half concealed behind a wall but she daren't move back into the shadows. Humans weren't nocturnal, their eyes not adapted for night vision like some of the Lathar, but even like this, human eyes were drawn to movement.

Even the slightest movement deep in the shadows could trigger the hindbrain and the survival instincts. It was a reflex she'd learned to trust as a marine. Depending on the situation, she'd either sweep the shadows with a torch or put a few bullets into them.

But neither Dex nor his companion looked her way.

Dex nodded. "Yeah, she will. I've got that one on the hook for sure. She'll do exactly as she's told. Especially when she's in my bed."

Asshole. She managed to bite back her growl, controlling her breathing. *Walk on by. You'll get yours. I promise.*

As they turned to go down one of the side alleys, she eased back into the shadows. The edge of her boot caught against a stone, crunching under her weight. It was the tiniest noise, but it sounded like a gunshot in the quiet of the alleyway. She froze in the middle of the movement.

"What was that?" Dex snarled, hand out to stop the other guy. "There's someone else here."

Shitshitshit, they were onto her. Instantly, Kenna's mind flashed through all the possible avenues of escape. But there were none that got her out of here unseen. Her hands clenched. The only way out was to kill them both. But they were armed and she wasn't. She also didn't have the element of surprise.

Fuck. She was screwed.

"Who's there? Come out now!" Dex ordered, fumbling at his belt for a torch. Before he could get it out, though, there was a sound from the shadows on the opposite wall. To Kenna's surprise, a couple emerged from them, looking all rumbled with their clothes in disarray. She blinked, recognizing them from the polyamorous group with one wife she'd seen before.

"Niall? Claire? What the fuck are you doing out here?" The tension eased from Dex's shoulders, and he slid his torch back away.

"Sorry, boss," the guy said, pulling the woman in against his side protectively. "Just wanted a bit of alone time."

Dex shook his head, chuckling. "Well, I'd tell you to go get a room, but I guess yours can be pretty crowded. Just keep it down out here, okay?"

"Got it, boss," Niall said, the couple turning to

walk away. As they did so, Claire looked directly at Kenna in the shadows and winked.

Kenna was so stunned, she stayed stock still as the alley cleared. Niall and Claire went one way with Dex and his companion going the other. They'd *known* Kenna was there and hadn't said a word. More than that, they'd *covered* for her. Why?

The mysteries about the colony sure were stacking up and getting more complex. But once she was alone, she put them in the back of her mind and continued. She made it the rest of the way to the prison block without incident, sliding around the back and pulling up a barrel so she could boost herself up and peer through the high, barred window.

"Pssst," she hissed, making out three figures— two men and the weird bot thing—slumped in the cells. "Pssst... wake up."

11

The sound of movement outside brought Xaan out of his light doze instantly. Stephens had fallen asleep a few hours ago, their small conversation seeming to have exhausted the Terran soldier. Probably due to his injuries. Human bodies obviously required rest to aid in the healing process, much like Latharian ones. It was yet another indicator of how similar Kenna's species were to his own. *Were* his own in fact.

He hadn't really believed it when Lord Healer Laarn had claimed humanity were from a lost Latharian colony expedition. He'd assumed that was just a ruse to get everyone, even the purists, on side to protect humanity from invasion by the worst elements of their society. A new species was fair game. A colony of Lathar? Not so much. Especially not one under the emperor's protection.

But... the more time he spent around humans, the more he realized that Laarn was right. Humanity were Lathar. They were so similar in some respects they had to be. There was no other explanation for it.

He sat looking into the darkness for a few moments as he isolated where the noises were coming from. They were very faint. Whoever was there was trying very hard to be quiet. Standing, he moved closer to the sole window, high up on the wall of his cell and barred like the front. He cocked his head to the side, listening. Yes, the noises were out there.

"Pssst," a familiar voice hissed as a face appeared in the window. *"Pssst... wake up."*

Pleasure burst through him at the sight of the human female—*his* human female—in the shadows behind the bars. He could see easily in the darkness but she couldn't, even though he stood right below her. Even with his superior height, he couldn't reach her, but he drank in the sight of her, searching for any sign of distress or injury.

Relief hit him when he found none. He'd been

worried that Dex would see through their ruse and hurt her.

"Hey," he murmured, moving closer. The movement drew her attention and she managed to focus on him, a smile spreading across her lovely face like the sun breaking across the morning sky. "You okay? You're not hurt?"

She shook her head quickly. "Marine, remember? Tough as nails."

Her reply was swift, but he saw the pleasure in her expression at his concern. She might be more than capable of looking after herself, but he knew she liked his protectiveness. He... may have overheard that in a private conversation between her and her friend once when she wasn't aware of his presence. Not his fault. They shouldn't have been discussing private things in a public corridor when anyone could overhear them, now should they?

But even so, no matter *how* he'd come by the knowledge, he wasn't noble enough not to use it. All was equal in courting and combat. Wasn't that a human saying? Something like that anyway.

"Yeah. I remember," he murmured, moving closer and reaching up. He still couldn't quite touch her but she reached a hand through the bars to help him and their fingertips brushed.

"How are you? Are you hurt?" Her voice echoed her concern for him, creating a warm and fuzzy feeling in the center of his chest.

"I'm good. I might not be a marine, but I'm plenty tough enough," he offered her a small smile, noting the way her gaze flicked over toward Stephens. Then he realized she'd kept their conversation light, not revealing anything that might hint to his non-human origins.

"He knows," Xaan said simply. "He's with us."

She nodded, just once, in reply. Message received and understood. Another thing he liked about her, she was blunt and to the point, rarely wasting time. "Okay, sitrep then. This bunch of assholes aren't colonists. They're scavengers."

One eyebrow winged up. "Scavengers?" He'd never heard the term applied to a group of humans before.

"Yeah. They prey on outer colonies, kidnap and kill the original settlers and take whatever's useful. I've never seen them actually settle a planet in place of the original group before but I think that's what they've done. There's an older, ruined compound a short way away." She paused and looked at him directly. "Mass graves too. Not just of the colonists I don't think. They have ships here. Looks like they're breaking them down for parts..."

He rumbled in the back of his throat, arms folded over his chest as he rubbed at his jaw. Stubble prickled his fingers. "That makes sense. The radio and beacons are all fully operational. So that means they are transmitting that message on purpose."

She nodded. "Yeah. To draw the unwary in. I've been pretending to break the encryption on your ship lock all day."

He chuckled. All she had to do was walk up to the ship and it would recognize her. They both knew it. "Have you now, little one?"

She wrinkled her nose at him. "I made pretty lights move on a screen. It was fun. Like playing old holo-games. There's something else. On my way here, I almost got caught—"

Fear ran through him and he straightened up instantly, but her raised hand stopped him. "No. I'm fine. But I think there's another group here that's not with Dex and his lot. Remember that poly group? The one with one female and more men?"

He nodded, remembering them sitting on their own in the main hall. "Yeah. What about them?"

"Well, two of them were out here when Dex almost caught me. They covered for me and I swear the woman winked at me." Kenna nibbled at her lower lip. "I don't know who they are but instinct tells me they're not with the scavengers."

"Another group?" That humans would prey on each other in such a way sickened him, but it was their reality so he had to deal with it. At least for now.

She pressed her lips together, thinking. "Not sure. I'll keep watch. I'm going to keep trying to reach the ship, or at the least get a message out on the main radio."

Snaking a hand through the bars again, she brushed her fingers against his. "You just hang tight. We'll get through this. Bye."

WHEN XAAN TURNED around from the window, he realized someone had been watching his conversation with Kenna. Stephens was awake, his expression thoughtful as he sat up.

"You two seem mighty familiar," he commented, unable to conceal his interest. For a moment anger and jealousy flared in the center of Xaan's chest. Kenna was his. *His*. No male, human or otherwise, would take her from him. "I didn't think you Lathar had any females of your own. That's why you're taking ours."

"She's not Lathar." Xaan shook his head, stalking the length and breadth of the cell. Unlike Stephens, he wasn't injured, so the enforced idleness made him antsy. "She's as human as you are."

"Really?" Stephens leaned back against the wall, cradling one arm against his side. Xaan couldn't work out if the arm or his ribs were injured. By the state of his clothing, it could be either. Or both. "And she's working with you?"

Xaan gave a small nod. "She came to the planet with me. We were investigating strange readings in this sector that shouldn't have been here."

He was starting to formulate a theory on that, but it would have to wait until they'd gotten themselves out of their current sticky situation. One problem at a time, he told himself. It was the key to survival in situations like this.

"Just work mates then?" Stephens' voice was light, but there was a note in it that made Xaan whirl around and pin the human with a hard gaze. He was getting used to their language. Work mates and mates were different things. The first meant just those a person worked with, had formed friendships with maybe... nothing to do with the Lathar use of the word as a soul and life partner.

"No. Not just work mates," he said, his voice harsh to disabuse the human of any ideas he might have that Kenna was available. He lifted his wrist to show off the blue ribbons, now faded and worn, tied there. "I wear her favors. She wi... *is* my mate."

Stephens eyes widened. "You guys are married? Hey! Congratulations!"

Xaan was about to argue that Kenna was not male, or a guy, in any sense of the word when he realized it was another oddity of the human language. They tended to group people together under weird terms, whatever their gender or defining characteristics.

"Thank you," he inclined his head. "Our bonding is very new." Like he hadn't claimed her yet, but he sure as *draanth* was going to. And soon. He'd already wasted too much time.

"So, you guys and humans can..." Stephens trailed off, watching Xaan with interest.

"We have compatible genitals, yes." Xaan's voice was gruff as he answered the obvious question. "Humans and Lathar are genetically related."

Surprise flared over the human male's face for a moment. Then he nodded. "That would make a lot of sense. You're very similar to us, at least... you are. Are you typical for a Lathar?"

Xaan chuckled. He was the emperor's champion. He was so far from typical it was unreal.

"Physically. Yes. I'm fairly typical for my species. My coloring is a little unusual," he admitted, running a hand through his short, pale hair. Blond, Kenna had called it. There wasn't an equivalent word in the Latharian language for it. Dirty yellow maybe? As far as he knew, only he and Rynn, his son, had hair that color. "Height I'm around average. Muscle mass, a little above."

He kept things factual, limited only to what Stephens could see. He didn't need to know where Xaan sat in the Latharian hierarchy. At the moment that would not help their situation any.

"Well, the ladies do love a ripped guy." Stephens managed a chuckle as he moved. The ribs were damaged, Xaan realized, not the male's arm. He was just using that to support himself as he shifted position, easing into a new, more comfortable one with a sigh of relief.

"They seek out a male in his prime for protection and for good genetics to sire their young?" He found himself asking, seeking an insight into human females from a different perspective.

Stephens shot him a look of surprise, then smiled. "Yeah, I guess you could say that. Although your gal there? She's a marine, right?"

Xaan nodded and the human carried on. "Yeah... thought I recognized the attitude. Your conversation just confirmed it. She's as hard as nails then, so she's not looking for protection."

"Her military training," Xaan nodded. That made sense. Even though he wanted to protect her, she didn't need him for that. She could take care of herself.

"Yes and no..." Stephens shrugged. "Some women are like that even without the training. Some women have the training and still look for a man's protection. It's not physical. It's a mindset thing. We have a saying... the female of the species is more deadly than the male."

Xaan folded his arms over his chest. "How does that work? Typically they're smaller and weaker than males. How can they be more dangerous?"

Stephens shrugged and then winced, holding a hand to his ribs. "It's not always about physical strength. We got loads of creatures where the female is deadly. Praying mantis—they're an Earth insect— they *eat* their males after sex. Bite their heads right off. And octopus? If the female doesn't want sex and a male bothers her, she'll screw him and then throttle him and keep him in her den for food. I think our women took a few lessons from the animal kingdom."

Xaan blinked in surprise. "I don't think I'd like your planet much. Sounds violent. How the *draanth* did your species even survive?"

Stephens grinned. "Because we're as stubborn as fuck. Tell us we can't do something and we'll trip over ourselves to prove you wrong."

A groan rolled up from the center of Xaan's chest, borne of memory and frustration. "Yeah. Dealing with your women, *that* sounds familiar."

Stephens laughed at that, a short bark of amusement. "Well, you lot were the idiots who took a load of fleet women. They're the most independent of the lot. You deserved everything you got. We had bets running, you know? That you'd probably bring them back and demand money or something. Like a reverse ransom."

Xaan's face split into a broad smile. "Yeah, we probably did. But you're not getting them back. Half of them are already bonded to our warriors, the others... well on the way to it."

His gaze slid sideways to the bot slumped in the corner next to Stephens.

"Okay, so what's the deal with that?" he asked, shaking his head and holding up his hand as Stephens went to speak. "Yeah, I know what you said. But it doesn't make sense. That's a worker model. It doesn't think on its own. It would have saved your life, yes. That's hardcoded into their subroutines. But it wouldn't have trashed the escape pod. The only reason it would have done that is to conceal its origins landing on a new planet not under Latharian control. But, that's an avatar action, not a worker one."

He moved to stand in front of the bars, looking down at the human male. "Then there's the obvious question. What were you doing on a Latharian vessel in the first place?"

Stephens watched him for a long moment and then sighed. "Because I was fucking dumb. That's why." He lifted a hand up to run through his close-cropped hair. "Saw something on long-range sensors while we were on patrol in the Clusters. It's an area right on the limits of Terran space, well away from you guys. Or at least I thought."

His expression shuttered over, the blankness of controlled grief in his eyes. "One of your ships picked us up. Weapons just sliced through our shielding like it wasn't even there and then they were in the ship. Four of my guys bought it there and then they dragged the rest of us aboard. Tortured us for days."

A chill ran through Xaan at the measured tone of the male's voice. He knew what torture was like, especially the Latharian kind. The fact that Stephens still had his mind said a lot about the guy. But what had he given up to save it?

"Thought I was a gonner, to be honest," the human male continued, only the slightest waver in his voice. "The others... they didn't make it. I knew I had to. I had to get back and warn command that there were more of your kind out there."

Xaan blinked. "Okay, having gone through all that, why are you even talking to me? I'd have expected you to try and get through these bars and murder me in my sleep."

Stephens laughed, a sound of amusement that became a rattle and then a nasty cough. "Yeah, right... in this condition? You could flick me and I'd fall over dead. Besides, just because I ran into one Latharian that was an asshole doesn't mean you all are. Does it?"

He sat upright, obviously trying to ease the pain in his side. He needed medical attention and soon. "I'm a professional soldier. Been in uniform since I was a snot-nosed teen," he revealed. "But I'm not stupid. Soldiers don't make wars. We just fight 'em. That asshole, D'Corr, he was the type who causes wars."

Xaan's gaze laser focused on him. "Wait, did you say D'Corr?"

"Yeah. Asshole with a big scar across his face. Why? You know him?"

Xaan nodded. "He's not Lathar."

"Sure looked it to me. Big, all that leather, those snazzy hair braids you all wear."

"No, no... I mean he's not Lathar now. He's what we call dishonored. Not one of us anymore."

Stephens began to chuckle but stopped himself in time. "You mean you threw him out of his own species for being a twat?"

"Yeah," Xaan replied. He wasn't sure what a twat was, but it sounded derogatory. "Pretty much. Okay, so you were on D'Corr's ship. Then what?"

Stephens blew out a sigh, looking confused. "That's where it gets hazy. There was a ruckus somewhere. Things started to go boom. Then she—" He nodded toward the bot in the corner. "Tore the front off the cell and hauled me out of there. I remember coming to in the escape pod and she told me it was going to be okay. Then waking up on the surface here with her and the trashed shuttle. That's it. Dex and his assholes got ahold of me then and I've been here ever since." Anger filled his voice as he looked toward the doorway they'd seen Dex last disappear through. "I kinda hope D'Corr lands here and wipes them all out. Would serve them right."

"Nice thought but not gonna happen." Xaan squatted down next to the bars to study the bot. It was motionless. No sign of life at all.

"Yeah? Why not?" Stephens argued. "They can't be far from here."

Xaan glanced up and fixed him with a look. "D'Corr's ship exploded halfway across the galaxy from here. I know because my son blew it up. Which begs the question as to how you ended up here with a Latharian bot that doesn't have a gender, but you say is female..."

12

"*I*'m sorry, but I can't break this."

Kenna pushed the small computer away from her across the canteen table, leaning back to shove her hands through her hair in frustration. It was keenly felt, but not due to the numbers she'd been shoving around on one of the settlement's hand-held computers all morning.

She had no intention of even trying to break Xaan's code lock on his ship and every need to figure out how to get into the colony's main office on the other side of the compound. Unfortunately, it was locked, the only key on Dex's belt. Which meant if she wanted to get into the office and to the working radio it contained, she needed to get the key from Dex.

The trouble was, even though he was trying like hell to charm her, he wasn't stupid. And he was very wary about those keys. She hadn't been able to get anywhere near close enough to lift them.

"Hey, hey... it's okay, love," Maggie dropped a hand on her shoulder in reassurance. "I'm sure you'll figure it out soon enough. Perhaps take a break, come back to it fresh?"

"Thanks, Maggie," Kenna murmured, squeezing the hand on her shoulder. Of them all, Maggie was the one she couldn't work out. She *really* wanted to believe the woman was on the level, was really the jolly, friendly grandmother figure. But here she was working with Dex and his lot—scavengers that had killed and looted. It just didn't jive in her brain.

"She ain't gonna do it," a harsh female voice announced from the other side of the canteen. Kenna let her eyes flicker half-closed, a look of frustration on her face. Bull-dog again. She hadn't liked Kenna from the get-go and had been getting steadily more vocal in her dislike. Mostly Kenna had tried to ignore it, but she knew she was going to have to deal with it and soon. Especially as the woman had taken to following her every movement. Which, given she was trying to sneak into the office, presented somewhat of a problem.

"Aislinn, you leave the girl alone," Maggie chided, her lips pursed. "She's got enough on her plate with that spy ex-husband of hers. Don't need you adding to her troubles, now does she?"

"Don't trust her," Aislinn muttered, glaring at Kenna again. "She ain't tryin' hard enough."

Kenna sighed, pushing away from the table and surging to her feet in a burst of movement. "Yeah, right? You got a problem wi' me, bitch?" she snarled, going from nice to street in a heartbeat.

Stationed on the lunar colonies of Tet-four early in her career for populace control, she'd seen enough of street gangs to last her a lifetime. But, it also meant she could mimic their hard-ass attitude like she'd been born there. So she channeled her inner street-hoe as she stalked toward Aislinn, getting all up in her face as the other woman stood, the chair clattering to the floor behind her.

"Because if you do," she snarled, "let's have it out here and now, shall we? Or are you too much of a yellow-belly?"

The other woman's manner had shut down, her expression blank and her eyes expressionless. She threw the first punch without warning, exactly as Kenna had expected her to. She blocked it and threw a punch of her own, slugging the woman across the jaw. Not as heavily as she could but just enough to sting and make Aislinn mad.

Bulldog stumbled back a few steps, her expression screwed up in hatred again. Good. Kenna needed her mad, not blank and emotionless. Mad people slipped up and made mistakes. Not that Kenna could win this fight, she mused as the two women prowled around each other.

Oh, she could easily beat Aislinn. She already had the other woman's measure and knew in a hands down fight she could take her apart in seconds. But... she couldn't afford to win. Aislinn already suspected her and to display that sort of fighting ability would ping too many people's radars. So she shut down her ego and concentrated on the fight.

She had to lose. But convincingly.

Aislinn moved in, and Kenna threw another right hook, catching the other woman across the jaw again. She ignored the fact Aislinn was wide open on the left side, instead dancing back as the woman staggered back a step or two, wiping her mouth on the back of her hand. It came away covered in blood.

"Oh, you're gonna pay for that, you little bitch," she snarled and moved in for the kill.

The fight became a flurry of blows and slaps. At one point Kenna got her hand in Aislinn's hair and gave it a good yank, only to be rewarded with a solid knee to the stomach. She doubled over, pretending to be winded, and caught an elbow to the back of the head. The blow was just off target to drop her but she went down to her knees anyway, pretending that it had. Aislinn needed to believe she'd won the fight easily.

"HEY! WHAT THE FUCK IS GOING ON HERE!" Dex's bellow stopped any further blows raining down on Kenna and she grabbed at the nearest chair to cling to, making a show of being dazed as the scavenger leader stormed across the canteen.

"What the fuck are you doing, Aislinn?" he demanded, reaching Kenna and pulling her upright. Settling her on the chair, he checked her appearance with a swift look. His arm around her supportively, he glared at the other woman.

"Suzie is a guest here. What the fuck?"

"She's a bitch," Aislinn's defiant attitude started to crumble under Dex's hard look. For a moment real fear showed in her eyes. She was scared of Dex. Interesting. Kenna would have put her down as one

MINA CARTER

of his core people. "She ain't who she says she is. I seen her before. She's one of them women the aliens took."

"W-what?" Startled, Kenna's reaction was genuine. How the *fuck* did she know that? Quickly she laughed, looking up at Dex. "She's off her rocker. How can the aliens have taken me if I'm here? Don't they put women they take in those evil breeding factories?"

It made her feel sick to even mention that vile lie but she had no option. She needed them to stop thinking along those lines. Right *now*. If Dex so much as suspected she was one of the Sentinel women, this would get a lot harder very quickly.

"Yeah." Dex's voice was hard as he looked at the other woman. "Those women were all marines, Aislinn. You know that. Does Suzie *look* like a marine to you? You just about beat the crap out of her. Would you be able to do that to a battle-hardened veteran?"

Aislinn shuffled her feet, her gaze flicking between the two of them. "No, I guess not," she admitted, a hard flush riding high on her cheeks.

"Good. Now get the fuck out of my sight."

The scavenger woman fled at the harsh order but

by the time Dex turned back to Kenna, his manner had softened. Concern filled his face as he studied her, focusing on the cuts on her cheek and by the corner of her lips.

"Come on. Let's get you cleaned up. I would apologize for Aislinn, but I think I'll make her do that herself. Publicly."

Kenna shook her head, her hand soft on his arm. "Please. Don't do that. She already doesn't like me. Humiliating her will just make it worse... especially if I'm going to stay," she added, playing her trump card. "I'd like to get on with everyone here."

He smiled, his manner relaxing as he helped her up out of the seat and led her toward the medical bay. "You really are too sweet. You know? You're gonna have to toughen up if you're going to survive out here in the colonies."

This asshole really had *no* idea. Kenna hid her amusement, playing up the injured and shocked woman as they left the main hall. If they knew the truth, they'd already have executed her. She'd be in a shallow grave someplace. Normally, she'd have grabbed whatever she could and shanked him on the spot, but... she needed him.

She'd been all over the settlement on a "walk"

earlier. Security had been upped, so there was no way to get out to Xaan's ship and send a message. Her only option was to get into the main office and send a message to the fleet from there.

But... it was locked. All. The. Time.

She'd watched it for a while, thinking she could slip in as someone left it. Not an unreasonable assumption; a colony's main office was the hub for everything. It usually had more foot traffic than an intergalactic space station. Problem with the hydropumps? Head to the office. Little Arnold had a boo-boo? Get yourself to the office to call for the doc. Planet-wide emergency like assholes attacking the colony? Get to the office. It was the hub that everything revolved around.

But no one came and went. The only person that seemed to have access was Dex himself. She'd watched as he'd locked the door carefully behind him as he left, sliding the keycard into his back pocket.

She had to get that key. But he kept turning away from her so she couldn't slide her hand into the pocket of his cargo pants without alerting him.

"Have you made a decision about joining us then?" Dex asked. He left her sitting on the main examination bed as he moved around the room, collecting supplies to bring back to the trolley next to her.

That was one notable absence she realized, sitting still as he cleaned up the cuts on her face. She even remembered to flinch as a civvie would. There was no doctor. She'd only seen Dex or one of his men in here, and none of them struck her as the medical type.

Of course, she could be wrong. Don't judge a book by its cover and all that, but in her experience the willingness to kill people and the Hippocratic Oath didn't jive well. Nor did doctors often carry assault weaponry.

A quick image of Laarn, and the other Latharian healers sprang to mind, going about their duties in combat leathers and armed to the teeth, but she squashed it down. *Human* doctors often didn't go about armed...

"Yeah," she nodded, looking away from him. "I'm staying. Got no place else to go, and why would I want to leave here? It's beautiful."

"That's wonderful news. I'm so pleased to hear that!" His smile was wide, genuine pleasure in his eyes. If he wasn't such a murdering asshole with a hard-on for stealing other people's shit, like their godsdamn *planet,* he would actually have been handsome.

He finished cleaning her up, tilting her chin up with a finger. "There we go, good as new."

"Thank you," she smiled as he half turned to deal with the blood-streaked dressings on the trolley. There, right in front of her, the key card peeked from his back pocket. Holding her breath, she reached out, quick as a flash and slid it from its fabric confinement.

By the time he turned to smile over his shoulder at her, the card was safely concealed up her sleeve. She smiled so sweetly she was surprised her teeth didn't rot on the spot.

"You're good to go, love. Are you joining one of the work parties this afternoon? Some of the ladies are working in the mill today. You could learn that part of the harvest if you like?"

She wasn't surprised at the suggestion, and the fact it kept her safely within the main walls. Despite all his pretty words about her joining the colony, she was a prisoner. Poor Suzie Renner hadn't realized it, but Kenna Reynolds knew exactly what was going on.

"That sounds interesting," she confirmed as she slid from the bed. Then she paused, faking hesitation to leave the room as she looked at him shyly. "Will I see you at dinner?"

"Wouldn't miss it for the world. Save me a seat?" he said, dumping the waste from the trolley into the recycler.

"Will do," she chirped and left the medical bay.

"OVER HERE. NOW, ASSHOLE."

Xaan sighed at the predictable insult. Two men stood by the door at the back of the room, weapons trained on him as Billy motioned for him to step toward the door of the cell. His injured arm had obviously been treated, the thick field dressings that had covered the wounds from the thorns replaced with smaller ones. They must have a flesh regeneration unit he hadn't seen while in the medical bay. His expression impassive, he moved to the front of the cell as ordered.

"Arms out. Don't try anything funny or these two'll put a bullet through your skull. Understand?"

The insults might have been predictable, but at least Billy was switched on, not taking chances where Xaan was concerned. Pity, he would have enjoyed introducing the human's face to the bars. Repeatedly. Especially now he knew from Kenna that these murdering *draanthic* had killed the original colonists.

Without a word, he lifted his arms, holding them still as Billy reached through the bars and slapped heavy manacles around his wrists, locking them to each other. He gave them a testing tug only for Billy to laugh as he unlocked the cell door.

"That ain't gonna do you any good, sunshine. They might look flimsy but that there's high tensile Quadtanium steel alloy. Not even one of your bastard alien friends'll be able to break it."

Xaan lifted an eyebrow as he stepped from the cell. Like a lot of humans, Billy was as xenophobic as hell. It didn't bode well for future human-Latharian integration. But then, he mused as the human shoved his shoulder roughly, pushing him toward the door, this group were *not* the sort of group his people wanted anything to do with. Yes, the Lathar might be a highly war-focused society but they were honor driven. Dex and his group were so far from any sort of honor code it was unreal.

"Out. Boss wants to see you." The order was rough as they herded him toward the door.

It didn't take long for the three of them to march him toward the main square of the compound. A small group had assembled in front of Dex and what looked like a big display screen. For a moment Xaan wondered what it was for, but then it flickered into life and displayed an image of his ship. Or rather, the human trader vessel his ship was pretending to be.

He spotted Kenna in the group as he was pushed to stand in front of them, but she avoided his gaze. Good, she was still keeping to her cover. He had every faith she would find a way to give them an edge. One he didn't have at the moment with two rifles covering him from different angles. Had the two goons with Billy grouped together nicely for him, he'd have made a play for one of their weapons, disabling one before shooting the other. But sensibly, they'd stayed well apart and far enough away that as soon as he made a move toward one, the other had time to put a bullet through his brain. And, while the Lathar might have a lot of advantages over humanity, a bullet proof cranial coating was not one of them. He'd be dead before he hit the ground.

He looked at Kenna again. And he had too much to live for to let that happen.

"Our guest arrives," Dex smirked as Xaan was pushed to stand next to him. "I hope you find our... hospitality to your liking."

He shrugged. "Bed's a bit hard and the food

leaves much to be desired. I'd sack your chef if I was you."

Dex laughed, his manner superior and smug, as though he knew he had the upper hand. If Xaan had been in his shoes though, he'd have been wondering why his prisoner was so calm and unruffled. But then, Dex *had* come across marines before, albeit wounded ones like Stephens, so he was obviously measuring Xaan by that yardstick.

Good.

"Now you've had a chance to think about it, I want to offer you the opportunity to do the right thing." He waved toward the ship on the screen. "Give us the access codes for your ship."

"No."

The word was blunt and to the point, dropping into silence. The crowd murmured as they watched the scene playing out. The eagerness on their faces sealed his impression of them. None of them were innocent. If they'd been part of this colony originally, they weren't now. They were Dex's people and complicit in his crimes. He noticed Kenna slip away out of the corner of his eye but didn't draw attention to the fact he'd noticed, instead focusing on Dex.

"I beg your pardon?" the scavenger leader spluttered.

Xaan's lips quirked. "No need to beg. It's not manly."

Dex nodded to Billy and pain exploded through the back of his skull as the human slammed his rifle butt into the back of Xaan's neck. He went down on one knee in response. Not because he needed to—the blow hadn't been that hard—but to keep up the appearance of playing human.

"Codes. Now," Dex snarled right in Xaan's face. He didn't need to bend down too far to do it, which made Xaan smother a smile of amusement. "Or we'll destroy your ship."

Xaan met him look for look. "No you won't. You need my ship to get off this planet."

"No we don't," Dex scoffed. "Why would we want to leave such a veritable paradise?"

There was no sense arguing with the delusional, so Xaan didn't. He just shrugged.

"Codes."

"Either you're deaf or stupid. What part of 'no' didn't you understand?" Xaan was thoroughly enjoying himself now. Who knew throwing human insults at humans could be so entertaining? "Should I use small words as well?"

Billy hit him again. This time he added a small grunt for effect and imagined shoving the *draanthic* thing up the human's ass. Sideways.

"It seems our spy here wants to conceal the evidence of his crime!" Dex cried out, playing up to the crowd around them. His eyes glittered nastily. "Let's disabuse him of that notion, shall we?"

He snatched the radio from his belt. "Karl? Blow it open."

Draanth. Xaan swiveled to look as the view on the screen changed. A farm vehicle trundled into view with what looked like a ship gun array mounted to the back. A male, presumably Karl, stood behind the heavy weapon.

"You might not want to fire that on the surface," Xaan began. "That looks like an orbital weapon." Aka something not designed to be fired in atmosphere. He didn't know about human weaponry, but with the equivalent Lathar version, it would turn Karl and his vehicle into a very pretty fireworks display.

Dex just grinned.

"Worried about your ship? Give me the codes and we can stop this all right here, right now."

"Worried you're going to lose your man and have another death on your conscience more like," Xaan threw back, looking worriedly at the screen but not for the reasons Dex thought. If the male fired that weapon so close to the *Jerri'tial's* shielding, the energy rebound would shatter the links between every cell in his body.

Dex clicked the radio. "Light him up, Karl."

Xaan closed his eyes. Less than a second later, an explosion split the air, making him wince. When he opened his eyes, the view on the screen was obliterated. He knew what they'd see, though, before the dust cleared from the air.

Karl and his vehicle were toast, a burning pyre in their place that stood in testament to Dex's stupidity. But the untouched ship behind it drew everyone's attention.

"What the..." Dex breathed, looking at the screen in utter shock along with the rest of the group. "There's no way it could have taken a shot like that."

Right on cue, the shielding on the *Jerri'tial* failed. It flickered in and out a few times, juxtaposing the sleek combat flyer with the image of the clunky trader, and then, with an audible fizzle, the trader was gone.

"It-it's..." Dex blinked, his mouth dropping open. "It's an alien ship."

He whirled around to stab a finger at Xaan. "Where did you get an alien ship? Tell me! Did they let you have it?"

"There was no *letting* me have anything." The game was up, so Xaan dropped all pretense. Closing his eyes, he disengaged the contacts that had concealed the true appearance of his eyes and looked directly at the human in front of him. "The ship's always been mine."

"Y-Y-You're one of them!" Dex whispered, backpedaling. "You're..."

"I am Xaandril of the Lathar." Xaan smiled. "And you wouldn't believe me how... what's the phrase humans use? Ah yes. You wouldn't believe me how *fucked* you lot are."

It took the scavenger leader a few moments to put himself back together. He snapped the radio up to his mouth. "Jason. Emily. I don't care how you do it, but blow that fucking ship to kingdom come."

Xaan watched the screen impassively as two more farm trucks, armed like the first, rolled into view. He didn't alter his expression when they started to fire on the *Jerri'tial*. With its shielding down, even its tough hull couldn't hold out against the sustained fire.

Within minutes, it exploded, the fire visible on

the horizon even from the compound. Dex grinned in triumph. "That's it. You're stuck on this planet with us now. Guards, take him away."

Xaan didn't move, a small smile on his lips as he locked gazes with Dex long enough to make the human look uncomfortable. "You've got it wrong. You're stuck on this planet with *me*. How do you think that's gonna work out for you, asshole?"

The snarl warned him a second before Dex yanked a handgun from his belt and jammed it against his temple.

"Really? I think that's gonna work out just fine once I've splattered your fucking alien brains all over the dirt."

Xaan didn't blink as he read his own death in the human's eyes. Regret filled him. Not because he was afraid of dying—he'd never been scared of his own death. After his first family had died, he'd spent years actively chasing it, only for the gods to refuse him that salvation. But now? He only regretted that he'd waited so long with Kenna.

"Pull that trigger," he said in an ice-cold voice, "and you hand down a death sentence to every human drawing breath on this planet."

"Yeah, right," Dex jeered. "You got a titanium

skull or something and you'll somehow survive me blowing your brains out?"

"No." Xaan didn't move, didn't break eye contact with the human. "I'll be dead. But my son isn't."

"Pffft, like I'm scared of your baby boy."

Xaan chuckled, the sound low and dangerous. "Oh, you should be. My 'baby boy' is the emperor's shadow... the most lethal assassin in the galaxy. You kill me and he *will* want vengeance. And that's before the emperor gets in on the act. Not one of you will survive."

He saw Dex's eyes shift, the fear leaching into the backs of them. Even out here, that name meant something.

"Not one. Even if you flee this planet, Rynn will find you."

The pressure on his temple eased up and then was gone as a commotion started up at the back of the square. Xaan and Dex turned to see one of the colony women marching Kenna toward them, a gun at her back. She shoved the smaller woman forward, Kenna half turning to retaliate. The muzzle aimed point blank between her eyes made her think again and she stopped.

"What do you mean by this, Aislinn?" Dex

demanded, anger in his voice. Xaan was forgotten for a moment as he strode forward.

"I caught her in the office, tryin' to send a message!" Aislinn didn't take her eyes off Kenna, hatred burning bright. "I *knew* I recognized her." She dug a small data-pad out of her pocket and handed it to Dex.

"She's one of them Sentinel women. The ones the aliens kidnapped. She's working with him."

13

She'd been a fucking idiot.

Kenna seethed with frustration and straightened to see the expression on Dex's face change at Aislinn's announcement. She should have known the other woman was keeping an eye on her, but even though she'd been careful breaking into the office, Kenna still hadn't spotted her. Not until there was a muzzle pressed in between her shoulder blades.

The damn bulldog must have been lurking somewhere out of sight, waiting to make her move. Kenna sighed. She should have expected something like this. Aislinn had had a thing against her since she'd arrived, and letting the woman beat her in a fist fight didn't seem to have mollified her. Perhaps she suspected the truth... that Kenna could beat her with one hand tied behind her back and blindfolded.

Some people just couldn't resist looking a gift horse in the damn mouth. Could they?

Dex's expression hardened.

"Who are you?" he demanded. Finally, she got a glimpse of the real guy behind the mask.

"Sergeant Kenna Reynolds." Her expression didn't flicker as she matched him stare for stare and dropped any pretense of being Suzie Renner. She nodded toward Xaan. "This is Xaandril. We're the advance scout for a human-Lathar rescue party out this way."

Dex frowned. "Rescue party? Because of that stupid little message? Don't lie to me. No way anyone's bothered about pathetic colonies out here."

She shrugged.

"You might think they're pathetic, but command doesn't. And there's not just your distress call," she lied, needing some narrative to keep her and Xaan alive. "These systems have been lighting up like a damn Christmas tree recently. Alien attacks all over the place. The Lathar say it's not them, so we came to check it out."

"Of course it's them!" Dex dismissed the idea

with a wave of his hand. "Lying bastards are after all our resources."

Gods, he was an asshole.

"We should kill them. Bury them out in the fields. No one'll ever know," Aislinn insisted, her eyes glittering as she leveled her gun at Kenna's head.

Xaan made a small sound, murder in his eyes as it looked like he was about to launch himself at the human woman. Kenna warned him no with a tiny shake of her head. If anyone was going for the woman, she was. She had a score to settle with her.

"Won't help, sweet cheeks," she told the other woman. "The Lathar can scan a planet down to the last molecule. They'll find us no matter what you do. And if you hurt either of us then god help you because no one else will."

"Crap*crap*CRAP!" Dex ran his hands through his hair, his expression tense and worried. She didn't blame him for starting to panic. So would she if she was faced with a possible combined alien-human force with advanced technology that could root out everything he'd been hiding.

"I need to think," he announced. "Get them out of my sight. Lock them up until I've worked out what the fuck to do."

They were summarily hauled away and frog marched back to the prison in the old workshop. The instant the cell door closed behind them, Kenna threw herself at Xaan, seeking the security and comfort of his strong arms.

"Oh my god, I was so worried for you in here," she admitted, her face buried against his broad shoulder. Closing her eyes, she savored the moment as he wrapped her up tightly and held her close, absorbing his strength and the comfort he offered. "I thought they might hurt you. Kill you."

"It was no easier for me in here, *kelarris,*" he said, his voice little more than a deep rumble in the center of his chest, "with you out there where I couldn't protect you."

She leaned back to look up into his face. "You feel you need to protect me?"

His face was half hidden in shadow, but she could see enough for the expression there to make her suck in a hard breath.

"No," he murmured, reaching up to stroke his thumb over her lower lip. "Not need. *Want.* I want to protect you, among other things."

"Oh?" She raised an eyebrow as the tension between them rose. "Elaborate."

The ghost of a smile whispered over his lips, and

his large hand flattened over the back of her hips to pull her up flush against him. She caught her breath as the thick bar of his cock pressed against her softer stomach.

"Oh, you know exactly what I mean, little one."

"Uh-huh." She raised on tiptoe to graze her lips against his. "Perhaps I want you to tell me," she breathed.

He bit back a growl, the sound hitting her right in the pussy. Heat spiraled through her body, threatening to spill out of control. "How about I show you?"

Then his lips crashed down over hers, parting them in one swift move for him to thrust his tongue past and lay claim to the softness of her mouth beyond.

Heat slammed into her like a shuttle at high speed. Months of suppressed feelings welled up and bubbled over. She moaned and wrapped her arms around his shoulders, rubbing her body against his. She wanted... no, *needed* this. Needed *him.* She had since the first moment she'd seen him, when he'd disarmed her in the middle of the imperial court.

The kiss got hot quickly. His tongue slid against hers, thrusting and sliding, and she whimpered again. Her pussy ached, clenching hard as she imagined him over her, filling her, thrusting and sliding in time with the motion of his tongue as he penetrated her twice.

Made her his.

"For fuck's sake. If you two are going to start banging, can you at least keep it down?" a disgruntled voice announced from the shadows. "Some of us are trying to sleep."

Xaan lifted his head with a chuckle. "Careful. Your jealousy is showing."

"Too fucking right," Stephens growled, sitting up as the couple broke apart. Before any of them could say anything else, the door opposite the cells burst open, slamming into the wall as three people walked in. Two Kenna recognized—Aislinn, holding a gun trained on the cells and Sami, clutching a medical bag with white knuckles. The other guy, armed like Aislinn and with a similar expression of hatred, she didn't know.

"Treat him," Aislinn gave Sami a small shove toward Stephens' cell. "Boss wants 'em at least able to stand for later."

"Later?" Kenna demanded, dividing her attention between the woman with the gun and the other one letting herself into the human man's cell. "What's happening later?"

Aislinn grinned, unholy amusement and sick anticipation in her eyes. "You fucking traitors are being put on trial. For being fucking spies."

Kenna laughed. "You can't do that. There isn't a judge on the planet. No trial will be legal."

The woman shrugged. "Legal enough for us, bitch. We don't need none of your kind sniffing about, gathering intel for *them*." She spat toward Xaan. "Fucking alien."

"Do you think we should tell her that humanity is descended from Lathar," Xaan said in an undertone meant for the hate-filled human to hear.

Kenna shook her head. *"It would only blow her mind. She's not intelligent enough to process it."*

"You fucking bitch!" Aislinn surged forward, eyes filled with fury as she lifted her rifle.

"AISLINN!" The guy with them barked out, command in his voice. "Remember what the boss said. Don't listen to anything they say. And if you kill them now, he'll be *pissed*. You wanna end up in a shallow grave with them?"

Kenna's heartrate had kicked up as the muzzle of the weapon had swung that way, sliding herself in front of Xaan. His large hands around her shoulders pulled her back to ease her behind him, a small look of reproach in his eyes.

Aislinn grumbled as she lowered the gun and she backed up a couple of steps, looking over at Sami to bark, "Hurry up. I'm coming out in fucking hives being near these two traitors."

"Technically," Kenna drawled, studying her fingernails. "I'm the only traitor. Xaan's Lathar anyway. Can't be a traitor when you're working for your own people and Stephens over there escaped from a Lathar ship." At least she assumed he had escaped a Latharian ship given his bot companion.

She hid her grin as Aislinn processed that little nugget of logic and simmered. Before she could explode, though, Sami finished in the other cell. A glance confirmed that Stephens looked a lot healthier and pinker in the skin as he sat upright.

"I'm done," she said quietly, not looking toward Kenna in the cell. She didn't blame her. The tightness across her shoulders and the tension in her eyes said Sami was scared. Perhaps she was worried the traitor brush would be applied to her as well.

"Some bloody friend you turned out to be," Kenna hissed, adding venom into her voice. "Fucking liar like the rest of them."

The hurt that welled in Sami's eyes as she swung toward the cell, her mouth gaping open, was replaced by understanding and gratitude as Kenna disavowed any link between them.

"Come on," Aislinn ordered, but her voice was a little kinder now as she nudged the other woman. "Ain't no helpin' trash like this. Best stay well away from them."

"Thank you," Sami mouthed over her shoulder as the three trooped out. Kenna sighed and sagged against the wall as the door shut.

"That was a nice thing to do," Xaan murmured, brushing his lips against her temple in a quick kiss before moving over to the bars that separated their cell from Stephens'.

"How you doing in there?"

The major pushed himself to his feet and stretched carefully.

"Yeaaaaaannngggghhhh." His reply disappeared into a drawn out sound as his back arched, arms stretched above his head for a few seconds.

She joined Xaan, watching the human man stretch. She knew the feeling, the need to be careful. The body could be a little confused after deep tissue reconstruction and healing, still convinced there was damage that would rip and tear if you weren't careful. Yet at the same time, the body *wanted* to stretch to test it was actually healed. It was an odd feeling, that was for sure.

He dropped his arms and gave them a small smile. "Much better. Still a little sore but the wrongness is gone. I'm good to go."

She nodded. He looked better. She suspected he'd had internal injuries, but that the healing had patched them up. They'd still need to get him to a medical bay though. Sami wasn't a qualified medic, so anything she'd done would be a rough job.

But... they needed to get out of here and off this damn planet first.

"Remind me I fucking hate colonies sometime?"

Done stretching, Stephens strode over and checked on the bot. He reached in under a ridge on the neck to press something and then looked at the faceplate and sighed.

"Still nothing."

"Hmmm," Xaan rumbled, arms folded over his chest. Kenna watched him as he studied the bot and then the cell around it. She recognized it as a worker bot but she didn't know anything about them.

Xaan nodded toward the side of the cell, near the bars. "Move it over there. Near to the power lines. It might be able to draw off them."

"How?" Stephens asked, grunting as he started to

drag the machine across the cell. Kenna started forward, concerned he'd reinjure himself, but Xaan stopped her with a hand on her arm. She didn't say anything. He was right. If they didn't get out of here, it didn't matter much if any of them were injured or not.

Still, she nibbled her lower lip as Stephens dragged the bot across the cell. She'd never tried to move one, but she'd bet they were heavy. It certainly *looked* heavy, leaving deep marks in the dirt floor. Finally, Stephens got it to the other side, leaning it up against the cell bars.

"You really think it can draw power without being plugged in?" she asked Xaan as Stephens threaded the bot's arm through the cell to rest directly against the cables clipped to the plasticrete wall. He stepped back, arms folded as they all looked at the bot.

Nothing happened.

Xaan sighed. "It was worth a shot. These models don't have charge pods. They need much less power than the avatars, so they just cluster near powerlines when they're low and draw from them. But our cabling must be different from yours."

He started to turn away when suddenly, a light flared in the bot's eyes and it sat up.

"K-K-K-k-k—k—k—" it said, the sound trailing off, and then it slumped back. Lifeless once more.

It had made them all jump but then Xaan crowed in triumph. "I KNEW it!" He hissed, fist pumping the air. "It was just low on power. Leave it there and we should have it operational again soon."

He grinned at them both. "Once it's powered up, it'll be through these *draanthic* bars in seconds and we'll be gone."

Kenna couldn't help but share his enthusiasm. With the bot operational, their shitty situation had improved. They'd be out of here before nightfall and even if they couldn't get off the planet, they could survive in the wilds until someone came to look for them.

Then heavens help Dex and his band of murderers because the Lathar sure wouldn't.

HIGH ON THE triumph of the bot starting to charge, Xaan had been feeling optimistic. Those hopes were dashed though when the door slammed open again a few hours later. Rob and three other men trooped in. One look at their faces said their time was up. He looked over at the bot, but it was still slumped against the bars, inert. No help from that quarter.

Draanth.

"Out! Now!" Rob spat the order as one of the others unlocked first Stephens' cell and then theirs. "And just in case you should be feeling heroic," he told Xaan directly as he pulled a handgun and pointed it directly at Kenna, nestled in his arms where they sat leaning against the back of the cell. "She'll be the first to die."

That threat killed any fledgling plans in a heartbeat. He wouldn't do anything that would potentially bring harm to his mate. He *couldn't.* Lathar just weren't hardwired that way. He'd protect her from everything, even at the cost of his own life.

"Up, up, up!" he barked as they got to their feet and then marched them from the cells and out of the building at gunpoint. Reaching out, Xaan took Kenna's hand as they walked toward the central square of the compound.

He heard the crowd before he saw them, the excited swell of voices as they anticipated the afternoon's entertainment. His jaw set, teeth clamped tightly. This lot of humans were assholes, every last one of them. His people were often brutal and ruthless, but they didn't revel in the punishment and harm of others. They used exile and execution yes, but they didn't *enjoy* it as some humans seemed to. And even exile didn't need to be permanent. Unless he was dishonored as D'Corr had been, a warrior could always earn his honor back on the arena sands.

But humans? These humans? They were well beyond dishonored.

"Aha! The prisoners," Dex announced from the clearing in the middle of the crowd. He was sitting at a table in front of them, Aislinn to one side of him and Billy to the other. "Bring them forward. Put them in the dock."

The "dock" appeared to be a spray-painted square on the dirt. It was so fresh he could still smell the wet paint, but as he looked, he realized there were older marks there as well. The square had been painted here more than once. It had been painted many times by the look of it.

"This court is here today to pass sentence on these traitors," Dex announced to the crowd, waving his hand at the three of them.

"Hey!" Kenna announced, her voice ringing with anger. "If this is a court, what happened to our trial? You can't sentence us without a trial and a judgement. That's not how a court works."

Dex gave her a hard look. "We do not need a trial to prove your guilt. You were guilty the moment you took up with... *that.*" He sneered toward Xaan. "So we're going straight to sentencing. Given the nature of your crimes, and the fact we do not have the facilities to hold prisoners of this severity long term," he addressed the assembled crowd in front of him. "I propose that the only appropriate sentence is... the death penalty."

"*DEATH!*" the crowd roared. "*Kill the traitors! Kill the alien!*"

Xaan's blood ran cold, but his training kicked in. He twisted his arm slightly, feeling the comforting press of the blade he'd recovered from his boot there. If he could get close enough to use it... get ahold of a weapon from one of the guards around them, he could perhaps hold them off long enough for Kenna and Stephens to get away. His life would be forfeited, he knew that, but his beloved mate might survive, and that was good enough for him. Perhaps the ancestor gods would smile on him and they'd meet in another life and have the happily ever after they couldn't here.

"Dex! Help! Medics!"

A call from the gates broke through the general chaos and everyone turned to see a group coming through the gates carrying a stretcher. There were gasps of horror at the sight and even from here,

Xaan could smell the blood. Whoever was on that stretcher was dead. They might still be breathing at the moment, but they were already dead. No one could lose that much blood and survive. He should know. He'd been there. It had taken the best healer in the empire and a *trall-load* of luck for him to still be breathing now.

"Darron?" Dex was on his feet in an instant as the group carried the stretcher closer. Most of them were covered in blood and their faces were haunted. "Oh shit, is that Tracey?"

"Yeah, we found her in one of the deeper mines," the guy at the front of the stretcher said. "Must have been some kind of accident with the face-worm cutting the rock down there. I've never seen it get someone this bad but..."

The stretcher was carried in front of them and Xaan froze at the sight of the woman's injuries.

"*Draanth,*" he breathed, ice running down his spine. He looked up, directly at Dex.

"That's no accident," he said, his voice dropping into sudden silence as everyone around them stopped talking, cowed into silence as they looked death right in the face. "You need to get everyone out of those mines *now* and we need to get off the planet."

"Yeah, right. You would say that," Dex snarled. "Like I'd listen to you. It's just a mining accident. That's all."

"*Trallshit,*" Xaan hissed. "There's a *Krin* on the planet, and if you don't listen to me, we're all going to die."

14

"*A Krin?*" Kenna whirled around as soon as she was shoved back into the cell, the two guards with them looking worried. "Are you sure?"

"Perfectly." Xaan's reply was short and sharp.

As the guard shoved him forward, he dug his heels in. The Lathar, while they looked human, were much bigger and far more densely muscled. If Xaan didn't want to be moved, some weedy-ass bully only brave when he hid behind a gun wasn't going to budge him.

He turned, looping one arm up and over, catching the guy's arm and weapon. Yanking the gun from his hands, the big Lathar reversed his movement and slammed the butt into the guy's face. Bone cracked and the human dropped like a stone.

Xaan whirled around to deal with the other guard but Stephens grinned, gun in hand and the other guard in a heap at his feet.

"Wondered when you were going to make your move." He checked the weapon in swift, efficient gestures. "Full charge. You?"

Xaan looked down. The gun seemed ludicrously small in his large hands. His brow creased.

Kenna smiled and took it off him, checking it over. "Just over three quarters. We're good." She noticed Stephens' look. "Their weaponry and combat methodology is different than ours. They favor single shot and close quarters combat with bladed weapons."

"Ahh," Stephens nodded as he stepped into his cell for a moment to check on the bot. Kenna could have told him there was no point. The thing was as dead as a doornail. "Makes sense. Seems a little... primitive though. You good going out there unarmed?" he asked Xaan.

The Lathar grinned and a second later a small, viciously curved blade appeared in his hand. "Who said anything about being unarmed?"

Stephens blinked in surprise and gave a low whistle. "Where the fuck were you hiding *that*? Wait, I really don't want to know!"

"You gotta watch Lathar for that. They're sneaky-ass bastards. Always assume they're armed. Even if they're naked." Kenna chuckled as she reached the door, peeking out. All clear. "We're good out here."

"Oh really? What would *you* know about naked Lathar?" Xaan growled in that sexy way he had as he stalked toward her. The possessive gleam in his eyes had her heart almost stalling right there in her chest. She didn't fight as he hauled her close and claimed her lips in the quickest, most devastating kiss she'd ever been given.

"You will *never* think about any other Lathar naked," he told her when he lifted his head, his voice rough. "Or any other male for that matter. Ever again. I forbid it."

"Whatever you say, big guy," she promised, smoothing her hands over his broad chest. "Can I imagine *you* naked?"

His hand spread out over the back of her hips as he pressed them against his own. She couldn't miss the thickening bar of his cock against her soft belly or the heat in his inhuman eyes.

"Hey, lovebirds. Mind if we move this along a bit?" Stephens' voice was amused. "And can someone please tell me what the *fuck* a *Krin* is?"

They both chuckled as they broke apart.

"They're apex predators with eight arms that like to eat their victims. Alive." The rough burr of arousal that had been in Xaan's voice a moment ago had disappeared as the manner of the general took the place of the lover—clipped and professional. "I think this one is young. That's why I didn't recognize the wounds on the bodies in the medical bay. It was like a youngling... When they have no teeth but they're under the gums and need something to..."

He looked at Kenna, a crease between his brows as he searched for the right term. He was doing well considering he was speaking English. Sure, she could understand him if he spoke Latharian because of her neuro-translator, but no one else would. So he was winging it, speaking her language.

"Teething?" she suggested, trying to figure what he meant. "You're telling me this thing is *teething?*"

"Yes!" He nodded. "It's developing its hunting technique and the best way to devour its prey for maximum enjoyment. They don't need to eat their prey live," he added for Stephens' benefit. "But they say the adrenaline and pain makes it taste better."

"Asshole aliens who eat people for a hit. Why the hell not?" Stephens' face set into grim, determined lines. "Okay, this bastard needs to go down. How do the Lathar usually kill them?"

"Either we put a full war team on the ground or we retreat to orbit and nuke the planet's surface. Neither option applies here."

Xaan looked out the door and motioned to Kenna to precede him since she was better armed. She threw him a grin as she took point. That was what she loved about him. He might be growly and all possessive-protective but he never once assumed she couldn't take care of herself.

They made it halfway across the compound, weaving between buildings to stay out of sight, when the screams started. Kenna snapped a hand up, the two men behind her stopping automatically, and listened.

"Up ahead," she said as Xaan and Stephens joined her in cover behind some barrels. "Between us and the gates."

"The *Krin*." Xaan looked up. It was late afternoon, the sun low in the sky. "They're normally nocturnal, but it's young. It can tolerate the light better. If it's in here, we need to find somewhere to hole up and wait the darkness out."

"Loop left?" she suggested, his grim manner worrying her a little. Not the hysterical type, she locked it down tight. "Come around the other side of the main building. It's made from parts of the colony ship. More defensible."

He nodded as screams of pain and terror filled the air. "Sounds like it's stopped to feed. Let's move."

The compound was a blur as they raced for the main building. They passed a couple of bodies, although that was too kind a word for the broken mass of shattered bones and gore.

"Dead. Keep going," Xaan confirmed, hand on her shoulder to propel her forward when she would have stopped at the third, still moaning. It was the older lady from the food hall. Maggie. "It's bait to make you stop. It's how they hunt."

She nodded. A second later they turned the corner and the door of the main building came into view. The couple from the polyamorous group were in the doorway, assault rifles in hand and grim looks on their faces. The instant the woman spotted Kenna, she waved.

"GET YOUR ASSES IN HERE!"

The three sprinted across the main square. There were more bodies but Kenna didn't let herself look. It was the stuff of nightmares. She knew even the brief glimpses she'd gotten would haunt her dreams for years to come.

They barreled through the doors, Xaan last, and

the couple slammed it shut behind them, dropping a metal bar across to seal it. The guy stayed by the window, his gaze sharp as he kept watch.

"Thanks for the assist," she said as she turned to the other woman. "Kenna Reynolds." Introducing herself, she held out her hand. "Xaan and Stephens."

"Gracie Shardlow. Pleasure to meet you properly now we're all using our real names," the woman smiled tightly as she shook Kenna's hand. Her gaze zeroed in on Xaan.

"You know what this thing is? How do we fight it?" she demanded.

"We don't." Xaan scanned the room. "We hole up, barricade ourselves in and wait for sunrise. It's young but feeding fully now. It shouldn't be able to tolerate the light once the sun comes up."

Gracie nodded. "Soon as we got in here, my boys started to secure the entry and exit points. It's about as secure as we're going to be able to make it."

"Weak points?" Xaan was sharp and to the point, his question more a barked demand. Gracie didn't take offense, just replied in the same manner.

"The domestic pods. Barricaded what we could and guarded. Medical bay I'm iffy about, but the windows are high and small. I think it would be difficult for that thing to get in."

Xaan's lips compressed. "Don't underestimate it. They're fast, intelligent and resourceful. Get someone watching those windows."

"On it." Gracie whistled to get the attention of one of her group across the other side of the room. "Jay... get someone on medical."

"Okay. Where do you want us?" Kenna asked, relieved that someone here had some sense. "And who the hell are you guys? You're not Dex's lot, are you?"

Gracie shook her head. "Fuck no," she spat vehemently. "Deep cover working for the Colony Commission. Command got wind of scavengers working in this area so sent us out. We dropped in like you, under the guise of traders, but Jay had a contact here after being undercover a few years ago. They never even questioned us. We were about ready to blow it wide open when you guys arrived."

"Huh. Sorry about that." Kenna winced. She knew how much it took to put together an undercover op. She and Xaan had probably ruined years of work.

"Oh, don't worry about it." Gracie clapped her on the shoulder, squeezing quickly before letting go. "If your guy knows how to fight that thing out there, I'd rather have you here than not. We'll get through this."

A bang against the door made them all whirl around, weapons raised. Dex's face appeared in the window. One eye was gone, his cheek a bloody mess.

"Let me in!" he wailed, banging on the door. "Oh god, it's out here. Let me in!"

The guy on the door reached for the bar to lift it, but Xaan was across the gap in a heartbeat.

"No!" He slammed his hands down on the bar, keeping it in place. "That's not Dex."

"LET ME IN!" Dex shouted, looking over his shoulder. His expression was one of terror and pain as he peered in again. "It's coming. Please, you gotta let me in!"

"Xaan?" Kenna asked, unsure. "He's right there. He's injured."

"That's the point," the Lathar replied, eyeballing the human on the other side of the toughened plexiglass. "Those are *Krin* sucker wounds. If it got hold of him, he's dead. That's not Dex."

Dex's face went slack. Utterly devoid of emotion. If he hadn't been begging and pleading with them a moment ago, Kenna would have thought she was looking at a corpse with its eye open. He opened his mouth and the voice that emerged wasn't Dex's but a hideous cackling sound.

"Ohhh cleeeeeever little Lathar. I'm going to enjjjjjoy cracking your skull open and feasting on your braiiiiiins. Perhaps I shall make you siiiiiiiing as I do!"

"What the *fuck* is that?" Stephens gasped.

"That's the *Krin*," Xaan confirmed as Dex rose slowly on the other side of the window. Only where his neck ended there was no body. Instead, there was a long, iridescent tentacle.

"*Ohmigod, it's using his head," a voice* behind them gasped in horror. Someone puked in the corner, the sound interspersed with low moans of terror. The higher pitch told her it was one of the women. Probably.

"Yeah? You just try it, you piece of *dranthing trallshit!*" Xaan called out. "And I'll rip your *draanthing* tentacles off and shove them so far up your defecation channel you'll be able to tickle your own *kernagstrito!*"

Stephens looked sideways at Kenna, one eyebrow cocked.

"He's going to rip its arms off and shove them up its ass," she translated.

Stephens nodded, looking satisfied. "The classics are always the best."

"Preeeeeeeeetty little snackzies, caught in a cage! Weeeee! I'm haviiiiiiiiing so much fuuuuuuun!"

Then the *Krin* was gone, throwing Dex's head at the window as a parting gesture. It hit with a meaty thud, leaving a bloody imprint behind. Kenna tried not to think about it rolling away like a football.

"God, aliens. No fucking manners," Stephens announced. "At the very least it could have taken its rubbish with it."

"Looks like it took out the compound office," Gracie said as she dropped into the seat next to Kenna to report. "Dave can just see it from one of the windows in his dom-pod. Says it went in there about half an hour ago and threw all the furniture out. Took a couple of bodies in." She shuddered. "Best not ask questions about what it's doing with them."

Kenna shook her head. Having seen what the thing had done with Dex, she *really* didn't want to know.

They'd been holed up in the main building for

four hours, since darkness fell, and they still had five to go before sunrise. So far though, so good. The *Krin* had wandered around the main building, hurling body parts and abuse at the few windows that weren't sealed up. For the first time in her life, she was grateful for the enclosed, claustrophobic design of colony buildings.

They were a one design fits all scenarios sort of thing, which meant thick walls to keep both heat and cold out and tiny slit windows to let light in, but not big enough to get smashed in bad weather. The plexiglass was toughened, able to withstand a level nine hailstorm or a sustained burst from a machine gun. Which meant there was no way the *Krin* was going to smash through any of them with someone's right foot or a jawbone.

"All other stations good?" Xaan asked, waiting for Gracie's nod.

Every way in or out of the building and attached pods was sealed up six ways to Sunday and back, with guards at every choke-point. On Xaan's orders, each guard had line of sight with the next, so no one was left without a set of eyes on their every movement. An *allatronian* mouse, the tiniest rodent in existence, couldn't have farted anywhere in the place without them knowing about it.

They'd turned the central tables in the main

room into a command post. The rest were cleared away, colonists sleeping around them on camp beds if they could. Some just stared open-eyed at the ceiling. Kenna had no sympathy for most of them. With Dex they'd been responsible for countless deaths, so the *Krin* descending on them seemed like karma had really upped her game. She just wished karma had given them a bit of warning, rather than getting bitten in the ass with the rest.

Looking around, though, she realized the level of their losses. Sami and Eva, the young girl she'd been determined to rescue, weren't among their number. Sadness filled her. If they weren't in here, they were dead. There was no way the *Krin* hadn't hunted them down wherever they were hiding. As far as she could tell, though, none of Dex's main men were in here either. Good. Murdering assholes deserved everything they got. Instantly she felt bad. No matter what they'd done, no one deserved the *Krin*.

"Dave says it took out the main office?" Stephens joined them. "There goes the radio then. And any hope of rescue."

Kenna shot him a look, warning him to keep his voice down as she cast a glance at those in the camp beds. There was a fine line between being realistic and being a Debbie Downer, and Stephens was stomping his size elevens all over it.

"Not necessarily," Gracie shook her head. "Not sure how much recon you guys got to do before this lot were onto you, but there's a—"

"—*junkyard.*" Kenna finished at the same time, smiling at Gracie.

"Exactly," the other woman nodded. "With the remnants of the ships there, we should be able to find something that we can cobble together to get a message out. At the least there might be a couple of escape pod transponders we can set off."

Kenna and Stephens nodded. She explained for Xaan's benefit. "All Terran ships and comms relays are preprogrammed to latch onto and repeat escape pod transponder beacons. If we set off a cluster, it'll ping up on someone's screen somewhere."

"And," Gracie added, "from what I saw of what they got in there, some of those ships are near complete enough we might be able to borrow from one to get another working and get off the surface. Dave's not bad as an engineer..." she trailed off, looking at them in question.

"Not me," Stephens shook his head quickly. "Give me a rifle I'm good, but useless with anything that requires a toolkit."

"I'm out as well," Kenna replied. "But this handsome fella right here... you were a science officer, weren't you, Xaan?"

He grunted, massive arms folded over his chest. The way he looked now, the sleeves torn off his t-shirt to make dressings for the wounded and all his tattoo-like marks on display, he looked as far from a scientist as he could get.

"I was. Jury-rigged a lot of *trall* in my time. I'll figure something out—"

His words were cut off by a scream from the direction of one of the pods. It wasn't a normal scream but the type Kenna had never heard in her life before tonight. A type she could go a lifetime without hearing again.

"BREECH!" someone yelled and the air filled with the sound of gunfire. The five of them were on their feet in a heartbeat, racing toward the dom-pod.

"Oh god, it's got her!" the guard yelled, crying and firing wildly through the doorway into the pod as they reached him. Kenna shot a look into the room and wished she hadn't.

The *Krin* was in there, in all its eight tentacle-armed glory. It had one of the women who had been on guard, tentacles wrapped around her in a sick parody of a lover's embrace. It held her off the ground, her arms flung out to the side. Her clothes and the skin of her abdomen had been ripped open, four of the tentacles disappearing inside her body. As they watched, two re-emerged with gobbets of flesh in the suckers on the end. The woman screamed as she watched her own heart pass by her face to disappear into the shark-toothed maw of the *Krin*.

"Soooooo deliciiiiiiious..." it crooned, stroking her hair with a free tentacle. "Tasty little human. I liiiiiiike humans. Want to eat moooooooooore of them. Snackziiiiiiies!"

Xaan stepped forward. Without missing a beat, he lifted his rifle and put two bullets through the woman's skull. The *Krin* screamed in anger as her brains decorated the wall behind.

"Noooooo... doesn't taste as gooooooood if theeeeeey're deaaaaaad!"

Its wails were abruptly cut off as Xaan hit the switch for the door. It slammed shut, cutting off their view of it feeding. "Seal this closed," he ordered two colonists who had joined them. "And pull back to the main section. Barricade and guard that door."

The rest of them trooped back to the command tables and sat down.

"How was she even still alive?" Kenna asked,

unable to figure out what she'd seen. Xaan reached out and took her hands in his, stroking his thumb across the back of her knuckles in a soothing gesture.

"It's how it feeds," he explained, his expression tight as though he didn't like the words coming out of his mouth. "It uses the tentacles to hook into its prey's circulatory and cardiovascular systems and replaces them, keeping its victim alive as it consumes the internal organs." He paused, a look of disgust washing over his features. "They say it makes the meat taste better. This one? It was playing back there. Learning how long it can stretch out a meal."

Kenna swallowed. "That's just... sick."

The big Lathar nodded. "It is. It's the reason we hunt them if they dare step out of their space without multiple visas and valid reason. If we find them hunting, every species in the galaxy comes together to eliminate the pod in question."

"Pod?" Stephens asked suddenly. "What... like there are more of these things?"

Xaan nodded slowly. "That's why we have to get off this planet. This one is young. It might be alone now... but where there's one *Krin*, more follow. Always. Especially if they think they've found a new, unguarded food source."

"Shit," Kenna, Gracie and Stephens all breathed at once.

"Exactly. We need to survive tonight and get off this gods forsaken planet. Then come back with ships and blow it the *draanth* to hell."

15

The morning was warm, a gentle breeze on the air as the sun shone down. Xaan stood on the grass and closed his eyes for a moment. With the gentle rustle of the grasses and the chirping of the native avian lifeforms, he could almost believe he was back home, readying himself to perform his morning *Diraanesh*. Like every warrior, he did them after each sleep cycle without fail. The movements and exercises stretched his muscles and conditioned his body, but doing them with grass between his toes was good for the soul.

The wind shifted slightly and an acrid smell filled his nostrils. He wrinkled his nose and opened his eyes. He wasn't home. He was on some gods forsaken human colony planet, looking at a mass funeral pyre for the victims of a *draanthing Krin* that had somehow found human space.

At least they'd survived the night, he mused, as Kenna's small hand crept onto his arm, her expression filled with sorrow and understanding as she looked up at him. He smiled and brushed her cheek with the backs of his fingers. She thought he felt pity for the humans whose remains were burning on the pyre.

He didn't. Not for most of them. They had been murdering liars who had preyed on their own species and didn't deserve to live. The goddess Tsaalina, Lady of Justice, had cast her judgement on them by allowing the *Krin* to find them. The only ones he felt pity for were the ones who had shown courage in helping to protect their fellows last night —the woman the *Krin* had gotten to in the domestic pod and a male it had tagged when it had managed to get a tentacle through a drain.

He'd cleaned that one up himself, refusing to allow the humans to see the little that was left of the body after it had been pulled through the drain grate. He'd only needed a mop and bucket. The male had sealed himself in to stop it getting any further— a sacrifice of honor and courage.

"Their names will be remembered by Tsaalina,"

he murmured to her in a low voice, resting his forehead against hers. Utter relief rolled through him that she had survived the night. If the *Krin* had gotten ahold of her... He shuddered, and then ice-cold fury at the very idea slid down his spine.

If it had killed Kenna, he would have gone out there, empty handed if necessary, and torn the thing limb from limb. Xaantar, a legendary warrior of his line, had done just that centuries ago when his mate had been slaughtered by a pod of *Krin* while he'd been off planet. He'd ordered his men to drop him on the surface with nothing but his bare hands.

He'd slaughtered the *Krin* without mercy, every last one of them, leaving their dismembered bodies on spikes around his former home. It became both a shrine to his mate and a warning for any *Krin* that dared to venture onto the planet. Statues of the scene were erected on all border planets with *Krin* territory as a warning of what Lathar retribution looked like.

He'd have done that for his Kenna. If the thing had hurt so much as a hair on her head, he'd have turned this whole fucking planet into a warning of what happened when anyone dared touch a warrior's mate.

She was more than that. She was *his* beloved. A

general's *kelarris*. He was the emperor's champion and his rage and retribution would eclipse even Xaantar's.

Kenna leaned against him, so he wrapped his arm around her. They had nothing to do for now. With the engineers left alive, he'd made a survey of the ships and technology available in the junkyard. They were in a better position than any of them had dared hope. One ship was almost complete, only needing minor repairs with parts that could be scavenged from others in the yard. Simple jobs that didn't need him to be there. The other engineers were far more familiar with Terran ships and systems than he was.

He pulled Kenna closer.

"You look tired, *kelarris,*" he murmured, brushing his lips against her temple.

She blinked and straightened up. "No, no. I'm good," she reassured him.

He hid his smile. She wasn't getting it.

"No... I think you need to rest." His voice was low as he pulled her to face him. Leaning down, he whispered against her lips. "I think I need to get you to bed."

"Oh!" Her little gasp was lost under his lips and he groaned as she opened up for him immediately.

Heat and need filled his veins as he pushed his tongue into her mouth to claim the soft recesses within. She inflamed him like no other ever had, and it took everything he had to stop his body responding fully. Only because he couldn't walk through the camp with a raging hard-on.

Pulling back, he looked down at her to search her expression for any hint she didn't want this. There was none. Instead, she tilted her head slightly.

"Well, what are you waiting for, warrior? Get on with the claiming already."

He grinned, the expression nothing at all to do with amusement, and scooped her up into his arms. She squeaked and then smiled at him as she settled against his chest happily. He strode back toward the compound. She fit there perfectly, like she'd always been meant to be there. He knew in his heart she had. She was his perfect mate, the one female who'd been made for him and just for him.

And it was time to make her his.

KENNA'S BREATHING SHORTENED, heat simmering through her veins as Xaan carried her toward their room. A flush hit her cheeks as others nodded to them when they passed, convinced they all knew what she and Xaan were about to do. The nasty, knocking boots, the whole nine yards... No, she corrected herself. That cheapened what was between them. He was a Latharian warrior claiming his mate and that was a beautiful thing.

Where she couldn't meet people's eyes on the way back, Xaan had no such issues. He looked at them all, nodding and wishing them a good morning but not offering any explanation as he strode past them with her in his arms.

"I think we passed bloody everyone on the way here," she whispered as he ducked through the doorway into the room and kicked it shut behind them.

"I don't care," he murmured. "You're mine. I want them all to know it. That way no other male makes the mistake of thinking he can steal you away."

As he spoke he slid her down the front of his body, his gaze locked to hers. Her worries about what people thought of them disappeared in a heartbeat.

She. Felt. Everything.

Every solid muscle and divot. The width of his broad chest, the cobblestone abs... the thick bar of his hard cock pressing urgently into her soft belly. A small gasp escaped her at his size, and the worry she wouldn't be able to take him filled her.

"You're mine," he repeated, bending his head to claim her lips.

The kiss could have rivaled a supernova for its heat. As soon as his mouth covered hers, he parted her lips with a hard sweep of his tongue. She moaned, parting instantly for him. His tongue slid inside in an urgent thrust to seek and tangle with hers. Months of frustration and need burst through her as she kissed him back breathlessly, her tongue sliding against his in an erotic duel.

He growled, backing her up against the wall nearest the bed. His hands were rough on her clothes, yanking her tank top up and over her head. His breath hissed over his teeth as he looked down at her in her bra. It wasn't the most seductive of garments, as plain as they came, but the dark heat in his eyes made her weak at the knees.

"I wanted this to be beautiful," he admitted, his voice rough as he reached out to stroke a finger along her jaw. It continued down the side of her throat, over her collarbone, and down into the valley between her breasts as he spoke. "I had it all planned. A meal at sunset, then I would wow you with conversation, then seduce you. Spend hours bringing you pleasure, making you writhe beneath me and beg me to make you mine before I finally claimed you."

"It sounds wonderful," she smiled and then hooked a finger in the front of his pants to pull him closer. "But hold that thought for when we get home. Right now, I just want you. It doesn't matter if we don't have a sunset and conversations..." She worked on his belt buckle. "I'm really only interested in one kind of conversation right now."

Looking up, she caught his gaze. "As long as we have each other, nothing else matters."

He nodded, the finger sliding between her breasts continuing down to toy with the clasp of her bra. He held her gaze as he pressed it. She bit her lip as he looked down slowly, taking her in.

She wasn't prepared for the reaction. A deep growl emanated from the center of his chest and he hauled her into his arms. His lips crashed down over hers as he lifted her and turned, tumbling them both onto the soft surface of the bed. Her gasp was lost under his lips as he kissed her, his lips demanding and urgent.

His large hand on her breasts, molding and caressing them, made her whimper, but not as much as when he fisted a big hand gently in her hair and pulled her head back to kiss along her throat.

"Xaan," she managed. "The cameras..."

"No office left, remember?" he muttered and then swept his tongue along her collarbone. Her belated protests disappeared under a shiver as she realized where he was headed. Body tight in anticipation, she closed her eyes as he trailed a line of kisses down her breast toward her nipple. His mouth closed over her, warm and wet, and she caught her breath at the sensation.

He suckled, and pleasure arrowed down from the beaded peak he teased straight to her clit. She moaned, trying to press her thighs together to ease the ache, but he was already there. His free hand slid down her body to tear at her belt and the fastening of her pants. They lasted mere seconds against his more-than-human strength.

She couldn't help the soft sound of delight as he lifted his mouth from her breast to tear her cargo pants and boots from her, leaving her in just her panties. His face tightened as he looked down on her, every line of his body tense.

"Beautiful," he murmured, the bed dipping as he put a knee between her legs and slid his hands up the sides of her thighs. Leaning over her, he brushed a kiss over her flat stomach and hooked strong fingers in her panties at the side. A shiver rolled down her spine as he pulled them slowly over her hips and down her thighs, lifting up as he did so to watch the expression on her face.

It was so intense, the simple move rendered so erotic by his focused gaze, that she trembled. She'd wanted this—*him*—for months, had fantasized about what it would be like but now they were here, it was *nothing* like she'd imagined.

It was so much better.

He pulled her panties all the way off before he looked down at her, his heated gaze slowly wandering over her revealed body. Dark heat flared in his eyes as he looked at her again finally, a large hand reaching out to spread over the outside of her thigh, strong fingers gripping a little.

"*Mine.*"

The growl was low and raspy, possessive and hot.

She bit her lip and nodded. "I've always been yours. Since you took that pistol off me in the courtyard when we first met."

"I've wanted you since then. The female who would blow a male's brains out for threatening her friend," he admitted, tearing his clothes off quicker than she'd ever seen a man undress. But not with desperation, instead he moved with utter intent.

She sucked her breath in at the sight of his naked body. It fulfilled the promise of the way he filled out his clothes, hard and heavily muscled *all* over. His cock was long and thick, flushed heavily with arousal. She was forced to bite back a whimper at the sight, utter need washing over her in a hot wave.

He crawled up to brace himself over her, a hand either side of her head on the mattress. "You were fierce and protective and I wanted that. Wanted *you.*"

She nodded, unable to say anything under the hot gaze he leveled at her. Her hands spread over his upper arms as he pushed her thighs further apart with his knee. Leaning down, he claimed her lips. The kiss was as hot and charged as the others he'd given her, demanding her response and surrender, and she gladly gave it.

Her moan when he slid one hand down her body was lost in his mouth, but they both heard it and felt the movement of skin on skin when she arched her back to press against him. She urged him on with movements rather than words.

Oh gods, he knew what he was doing. The thought burst through Kenna's mind as he pushed a hand between her thighs. Strong fingers slid between her pussy lips, a growl at the hot wetness he found there rumbling through his chest. Then he focused on her clit and she was forced to cling to him.

It was no hesitant touch, nor was it exploratory. He found the tiny nub and focused on it with singular intent, the wide pad of his finger slipping and sliding over it as he rubbed and stroked. Somehow he knew exactly how and where to touch her, bringing her simmering arousal into a full-blown inferno in seconds. She gasped and writhed against him, unable to stop the slight rock of her hips.

Then he pushed a finger deep inside her, the thick digit penetrating her in a slick, tight ride to stroke nerve endings within. She cried out as he pressed his thumb against her clit as well, tearing her lips from his to press her face against the strong column of his throat.

"That's it," he murmured as she trembled in his arms, on the edge of climax. "Come for me, beautiful. *Now.*"

The order rumbled in his gorgeous deep voice did it for her. As he pumped his finger within her, pressing against her clit again with his thumb, she cried out softly against the side of his neck and shattered.

Pleasure rolled through her in an unstoppable wave, a swell of hot, wet warning followed by what felt like a starburst low in her belly and between her thighs. Her clit ached savagely, her pussy clamping down on his fingers deep inside her as he added another, fucking her with them as she rode his hand. She panted and gasped through it as he stretched her pleasure out, her body his to play with.

Finally she came down, nestled against him as aftershocks ran through her system. He pulled his hand from her, sliding his fingers into his mouth and rumbling deep in his chest.

"Gods, you taste so good. Soon I'll have that as well," he promised as he moved over her, reaching between them to readjust himself. Her eyes popped open to find him watching her as he fit himself against the entrance to her body. A shiver of nervousness rolled through her. He was so fucking big.

He leaned down to brush a kiss over her lips. "I'll be gentle. I promise."

She moaned at the taste of herself on his lips and shook her head. "Screw gentle," she declared, grabbing his hips. "I won't break. Just... please, Xaan, I need you. *Now!*"

His growl fed her arousal, and he started to push,

rocking his hips against hers. They both gasped when he breached her, the delicate entrance to her pussy stretched wide around the thick, wide head of his cock.

"Oh gods," he groaned. "You're so tight."

"Just keep going," she panted, wrapping her legs around his lean hips to urge him on. More than anything she wanted him buried to the hilt inside her. She needed to feel him filling her. "Please, Xaan, I need you…"

"I'm here," he whispered, his voice raspy as he kissed along her neck. His hips rocked again and with each push, he slid another couple of inches in. She whimpered and bit her lip each time, feeling the stretch and burn.

And it felt so *good*.

Then he was in her fully, his balls pressed against her ass, and she chuckled.

He lifted his head to look at her.

"Is something amusing, female?" he mock-glowered, but she saw the smile flirting with the corners of his lips.

"You have balls," she couldn't help herself, biting her lip to stop her giggles. "Aliens have balls."

"Yes, we do." He claimed her lips in a hard, fast kiss of triumph. "And you saying that pleases me."

"Huh? Why?" She didn't follow the logic but then her ability to think was compromised as he began to move slowly, watching her carefully as if to see if she was in pain. She wasn't. Even filled more than she'd ever been filled in her life, it felt good. He was so big and the fit was so tight, she felt *everything*.

He grinned, speeding up a little. "It means you haven't thought about whether we do or not, which means you haven't thought about sex with any other Latharian male. That's good because you're mine. I'd kill any other male for being anywhere near you."

The sheer male arrogance had her smiling in response. "Oh yeah? Perhaps I never thought about alien balls because I was thinking about human guys. Ever thought about that, handsome?"

His reaction was swift and ruthless. With a growl he captured her wrists and hauled them up above her head.

"You will not think about human males either," he ordered, pulling back so he could slide into her in one hard thrust. She moaned at the sensation, almost ready to come again just from that one stroke alone. Bloody hell, what had he done to her?

"You will only think about me," he continued, his thrusts shaking the bed so much it slammed against the wall repeatedly. "I'll prove Lathar males are better. That *I* am better than any human male. I will drive them all out of your mind and you will scream *my* name in pleasure for the rest of your life."

"Oh god, *yes!*" she moaned, moving with him as he took her harder. The Lathar might not be much into romance and far more into claiming what they wanted, but *hell* did they know how to fuck a woman.

It didn't take him long, his powerful body moving over hers in a single-minded mission to bring them both pleasure. She moaned and writhed under him and then stiffened as ecstasy exploded through her again. She screamed his name as she came, hard and fast. She was followed only a few moments later as he stiffened and howled in triumph when he came, his thick cock jerking and pulsing as he bathed her inner walls with his white-hot seed.

She panted as she came down from their mutual high, her fingers gentle on the back of his neck. She could still feel the heat of his release and, for a split second, wondered if she'd be one of the females compatible with the Lathar. Images of a tiny little Xaan running around with his blond hair and her dark eyes made her yearn with longing. She wanted that. The whole nine yards, two point four kids and everything. With him.

He turned his head and claimed her lips in a long, sensual kiss she felt all the way down to where her toes curled.

"You're mine, Kenna Reynolds," he broke away to whisper against her lips. "And I'm going to spend the rest of the day, and our lives, proving it."

She smiled, wrapping her arms around his shoulders. "Good. Hop to it, soldier." But she gasped when he pulled back and started to move again, her eyes widening. "No way. Not already."

He grinned. "Not human, remember? We Lathar have a LOT more stamina."

And he spent the rest of the day proving just that.

16

*H*e was mated. Finally and truly.

Xaan smiled to himself as he stood in front of the ship with the other survivors and then belatedly realized the room was silent. They were all looking at him.

"Back with us?" Dave asked with a knowing smile.

He'd seen Xaan carrying Kenna back to their room this morning, so he had to have a good idea how they'd spent their day. Xaan nodded, ignoring the smiles from the group around him. At least none of them seemed to have issues with a Lathar warrior claiming one of their women. If anything, they seemed pleased for them.

"What do we have?" he nodded and asked, looking at the ship in front of them.

Short and squat, its body was bulbous but there were odd areas of a different color, all different colors actually, and none of them matched. Its cockpit screen sat off center and slightly slanted, and one of the landing struts didn't match any of the others, making it list to the side.

He frowned, rubbing his stubbled jaw. No expert on human ships by any stretch of the imagination, he had no idea what to say. It looked like the bastard love-child of at least five different ships and ugly as *draanth*. But what did he know? It could be cutting edge design or fine art as far as the group of humans around him were concerned.

"Meet Frank," Dave announced, his voice as proud as if he were introducing his firstborn.

"Frank?" Xaan's eyebrows winged up as he searched his memory for everything he knew on human ship classes. "Its class designation?"

The humans all chuckled, even Kenna.

"Nah." Gracie grinned. "No class. It's a frankenship... made up of lots of others and fugly as sin. Hence... Frank."

"O...kay... whatever you say."

Humans. He'd never understand them.

"Just a few tweaks to do in the morning. Then she'll be good to go," Dave said, casting a nervous glance at the sky outside. It was late afternoon sliding toward evening, and they were all aware that they were on the clock.

"And we'll all get in there?" Stephens wanted to know, eyeing Frank.

It was a valid point. Frank was only the size of a small troop carrier.

"It'll be a squeeze, but it'll take all of us," Dave smiled tiredly. Beneath his smile lurked the awareness they all shared. After another night with the *Krin* hunting them, the group left in the morning to board Frank and escape might be significantly smaller.

With that sobering thought, they turned to head back to the main building. Another team had spent most of the day shoring up the defenses as those who would stand guard tonight slept. Xaan, Kenna and Stephens had gone over them before coming out here to see Frank. Hopefully they would hold another night and then they could escape.

They'd barely made it ten steps from the front of the hangar when a sibilant drawl surrounded them.

"Loooooook at all the preeeeeetty snackziiiiiiiiiiies. So yum! Waiiiiiting for meeee!"

"CONTACT!" Stephens roared, all those armed in the group swinging around, weapons raised as they formed a protective circle around the others.

"Where is it?" Kenna called from one side. "Does anyone have eyes on?"

Xaan scanned their surroundings, human assault rifle feeling tiny and insignificant in his hands. *Draanth* what he'd give for a series KT-seventeen right about now. The big shoulder canon would give the *trall* something to think about. Take a couple of limbs off for sure.

"Two o'clock," he shouted, spotting movement and firing at the same time. There was a skitter and a giggle as tentacles disappeared into the shadows. *Draanth.* He should have accounted for it being young. It could be active far earlier, during the daylight that would paralyze an adult.

"Back into the hangar! Secure the doors! *GOGOGOGO!*" he bellowed as he walked backward. The rest of the guards followed his lead, forming a rear-guard action as the group fled back to the dubious safety of the hangar.

Xaan jumped for the huge double doors at the front of the building, a distance easily twice his height. His hands caught the bottom edge.

"Kenna! The motor!"

She got what he meant immediately, lifting her rifle. The sharp retort of gunfire was followed by a small explosion and then the rattle of the doors as Xaan's weight brought it down faster than the archaic motor would ever have been able to.

His boots hit the ground and he slammed the door shut. The *Krin* screamed, slamming into the other side of the door. Tentacles snaked underneath.

"Fuck off, asshole."

"Not on my *watch!"*

Kenna, Gracie and Stephens surged forward, all firing point blank at the tentacles. The *Krin* screamed in pain this time, yanking its appendages back. Xaan shoved the door down the rest of the way and slid the locking bar through the loop.

"That's not going to hold it long," he warned aloud.

He didn't need to vocalize the thought that the hangar was not defensible. From the terrified looks of the group, they knew that the *Krin* was getting in at them, and fast. They couldn't defend the hangar against it.

"Onto Frank!" Dave yelled, grabbing a toolbox.

Xaan and the rest with rifles formed a protective ring as the others scrambled onto the ship, Dave and the other engineers following them. If they could do what needed to be done quickly enough, they might just make it off the surface alive.

"*GET ON THE SHIP!*" he bellowed at Kenna as the Krin ripped the front door away in a squeal of tortured metal. It screamed a battle cry as it rose to its full height, all eight of its arms waving in the air.

"Now *that* is fucking ugly," Kenna breathed, coming to stand on one side of him while Stephens and Gracie flanked him on the other.

"What the *draanth* are you lot doing?" he snarled, firing strategically at the *Krin's* tentacles as it stomped toward them. "Get on the fucking ship and go!"

"Dropping the f-bomb now, alien? We're rubbing off on you," Stephens chuckled, firing at the *Krin's* knees. The bullets slammed into the left joint and the creature went down, snarling at them. Reaching out a tentacle, it grabbed a welding machine and hurled it at their heads. They ducked, just in time as the machine buried itself in the wall behind them.

"*You* don't get to rub anything on me, you sick *draanth,*" Xaan threw back, finding comfort in the familiar patter of warriors, obviously the same the galaxy over. "Only *she* can."

"*She's* the cat's mother," Kenna's voice was grim as she targeted the other knee. The joint blew and dumped the *Krin* on the floor. But it kept coming, beady eyes focused on them as its multi-toothed maw clicked hungrily. "And I'm not going anywhere. This sick squid-fuck is going *down!*"

"*SHIP! NOW!*" he ordered, and she flipped him off.

"Not a chance, handsome. It's both of us or not at all. So let's waste this fucker."

The four of them advanced on the *Krin* as one, splitting off to surround it.

"Target the brain ganglion at the base of the neck. It's too young for its armor to have hardened," Xaan ordered as their bullets picked it apart bit by bit. It snarled and lunged at them, using one of its tentacles coiled at the back of its neck to protect the vulnerable ganglion. But they were whittling it down. In its youth and inexperience, it had taken on an enemy it couldn't defeat.

Hope and triumph began to fill Xaan. They might actually do this. They might actually get out of this alive.

But as though the goddess of fate had heard him, she punished him for his premature optimism. A tentacle lashed out from the injured *Krin*, slamming into the center of Kenna's chest. She grunted, dropping her weapon to the floor as her skin turned a sickeningly pale shade. Blood welled up from the suckers on the end of the tentacle and splattered on the floor as the creature lifted his mate off her feet.

"*NOOOO!*" he screamed, lifting his rifle to aim right between its eyes.

"*Shoooooooot and she diiiiiiiiiies!*" the *Krin* warned him, waving Kenna in the air. "*I'll smash her into biiiiiits. Break her into piiiiiieces. Too many for to be put baaaaaaak!*"

"Stop!" he ordered, waving Gracie and Stephens off. Ice rolled down his spine as he frantically tried to think of a way to save her.

"Go." The whisper caught his attention and he looked up to find Kenna watching him, still aware despite the grievous wound the *Krin* had inflicted. Her hand moved against the holster at her side, fluttering against the flap, and he knew what she was going to do. Kill the thing as it ate her alive.

"Please," he whispered, shaking his head as his world threatened to collapse around him. "Don't. Gods, please don't."

He looked at the *Krin*. "Let her go. Take me instead. I'm bigger, I'll last longer."

"*You! Yooooou!*" the *Krin* crooned, surging toward him eagerly. It threw Kenna away like a piece of trash, but he didn't have time to see where she fell as the foul alien wrapped its tentacles around him. He didn't flinch as it drew him toward its maw, waiting for the bite of its sucker teeth as it ripped him apart. His death didn't matter. All that mattered was Kenna would survive.

"I hope I give you the *diaareental!*" he spat.

A shadow fell over him and he had a brief glimpse of red eyes. In the next heartbeat the *Krin* was ripped away from him. Shouts of alarm filled the air but no gunfire. He staggered a few steps, realizing that the *Krin's* sucker pads were still attached to his body. They just weren't attached to the *Krin* itself anymore, the torn and bloody ends flapping against him.

He grabbed them and ripped them off, throwing them away from him in disgust. Then he looked up and his jaw dropped. The worker bot had the *Krin* in a metal embrace, one arm around the thing's middle so hard that green blood seeped over onto its plating.

"Fucking foul thing," it said in a clear, female voice. "Did no one ever teach you to play nice?"

Pulling its arm back, it bunched its fist and drove it viciously into the ganglion at the back of the *Krin's* neck. The predator screamed and clicked its maw, thrashing to try and shake the bot off. But it was relentless. With a grunt, it yanked its hand back, pulsating ganglion and all.

"You're done, asshole," it hissed, showing the *Krin* its own brain matter.

"*Noooooo...*" the wail trailed off and became silent as the thing slumped in the bot's arms. Dead.

Silence reigned for the longest moment as Xaan and the two humans stared at the bot and the dead alien. It shuddered and dropped the thing on the floor, lifting a heavy metal foot to obliterate what was left of the *Krin's* skull.

"Kenna!" Xaan gasped, throwing himself across the room toward where she'd been thrown.

He found her under some barrels, slumped on her side.

"*Nonono*, sweetheart," he crooned, turning her onto her back. Her eyes were closed and she looked lifeless. "Stay with me. Please, gods, stay with me."

Her eyelids fluttered and slowly she opened her eyes. "Hey, handsome," she rasped. "What's a nice boy like you doing in a place like this?"

He managed a smile as he pressed a hand to the center of her chest, frantically looking around for something to stem the bleeding. Gracie dropped down next to him, a medkit in one hand. She held out a field dressing in the other.

He took it with a look of thanks, fear for Kenna running through his veins as he pressed the thing into place. He didn't need to be a healer to know the wound beneath didn't look good at all. It wasn't a "slap a bandage on it and keep her still until they were rescued" kind of wound. It was a "needs surgery ASAP" sort of injury.

"Are there any of your healers left?" he asked Gracie in a low undertone.

Hope died when she shook her head. He closed his eyes, dropping his head forward for a second as his throat closed over. Without a healer, his love wouldn't last another hour. Less from the blood pooling under her body. Agony sheared his heart in two. They'd only just found each other, now to have her ripped away...

"Hey."

Kenna's soft touch on his wrist made him look up at her. Despite the pain he could see in her eyes, she smiled at him.

"I'm here, *kelarris.*" He leaned in to place a soft kiss on her forehead. "Don't you worry. We'll get you fixed up right away. You'll be fine."

"Sure I will," she nodded but he knew she didn't believe him. She was just humoring what he desperately needed to believe. "Look."

She tapped his wrist again and he froze. Curling lines decorated the previously unmarked skin.

"Neat tats, dude," Gracie leaned in. "I didn't notice them before."

"Mating marks," he said, his voice cracking as he pulled Kenna into his arms. He needed to hold her. Needed to touch her. He couldn't imagine his life without her. He had been so convinced they had all the time in the universe, but she was being snatched from him before their life together could even begin. "They only appear when we find that one special person. The person we're supposed to spend the rest of our lives with."

Gracie nodded, but he saw the pity she quickly concealed.

"I-I'll go and see if anyone has any medical experience we missed," she murmured, leaving them alone.

"I love you, Kenna," he whispered, keeping his hand on the dressing in the center of her chest as he rocked her soothingly. "Always. I always have. I can't—"

He'd been going to say he couldn't go on without her, but he couldn't. His voice broke as completely as his heart.

"I love you too. And I'll always be with you," she

said softly, wrapping her hand around his wrist. Her touch was cold, her grip a fraction of what it had been. She smiled weakly as she looked up at him. "I was bought up to believe this life isn't it. We're reincarnated. Our souls come back. We'll see each other again, in another life. We'll fall in love and have our happily ever after. I promise."

He couldn't breathe, couldn't answer, so he just nodded as he fought to stop tears rolling down his cheeks. He didn't want the last thing she saw to be a warrior who couldn't control his emotions.

"Let me take her," a metallic female voice said.

He looked up in confusion to find the bot standing there, red eyes focused on them. It was wet, Stephens behind it with a hose saying he'd washed the *Krin* blood off.

"If you want her to live, let me take her," it repeated with a level of irritation not normally found in a mindless bot. "We don't have time to piss about. *Draanth,* you're as slow as your son. I practically had to kick him off the D'Corr vessel before it blew."

Xaan frowned, and then his eyes snapped open wide at the same time, almost causing facial paralysis. He'd heard the story of Rynn and the

D'Corr ship explosion and finally all the pieces fell into place. "*Keris?*"

Hope hit him hard and fast. Keris was an advanced AI, with more medical files in her databanks than any healer could hope to memorize. She could save Kenna.

"Live and not-so-much in the flesh." The bot reached down and gently lifted Kenna. The human woman had dropped into semi-consciousness, giving only a slight moan as she was moved. Keris turned and stomped toward the center of the hangar. "I need a table over here and whatever medkits you can find! And I'm going to need a uni-donor."

Xaan followed, already stripping his shirt off. "I'm uni level nine," he announced. "Retyped during early training for battlefield transfusion."

"Good." The big bot laid the injured woman down on the table Stephens and Gracie put into place. "Jay. Can you put a transfusion line in on Xaan please? A live one, we're going to use his heart to pump the blood."

Xaan blinked. "Ohh, it's Jay now?" he commented, realizing that Keris was talking to Stephens.

The marine moved quickly, kicking out a folding chair for Xaan to sit down in and ripping open the medkit to find the line. "This is gonna hurt," he warned. "No time."

Xaan shook his head as he dropped into the chair. He didn't care if they drained him completely. "Do it."

Stephens straightened his arm and tapped for a vein. Xaan hissed as the needle punctured his skin, the lines starting to fill with blood. He didn't bother watching them, looking instead to where Keris hunched over Kenna.

She reached out a metal hand for the lines, delicate auxiliary arms and hands unfolding from compartments in the side of her bot's body. As they watched, the hands started to move, peeling the dressing away carefully and then moving almost faster than the eye could see.

"What the hell is she?" Stephens asked, awe in his voice as they watched the bot operate on Xaan's unconscious mate.

"Illegal," he grunted, sliding a little in the seat when he felt the draw on his circulatory system as the lines pulled blood to replace what Kenna had lost. He'd been retyped during his early career so he could be used as a blood bank. Once tapped in, his body produced blood at an increased rate to replace what was drawn off. It could be the difference between life and death on the battlefield, unless he was injured himself. Then the ability switched off to save his life. It also gave him a blinding headache. But he didn't care. They could explode his head as long as it saved the woman he loved.

"Keris was the AI on my son's ship," he explained. "Sacrificed herself by piloting a ship set to self-destruct, D'Corr's ship, away from the one Rynn and his mate were on. She should have been destroyed with it."

"I was on D'Corr's ship." Stephens sat down next to Xaan and reached out to take his wrist, checking his pulse.

Xaan nodded. "Keris must have registered your presence and downloaded into a bot body to get you off the ship. She's hardcoded to save Lathar lives... or human it seems."

"So how is she illegal?" the human asked curiously.

"AIs are forbidden to download into avatar bodies. One went loco years ago and massacred a lot of people."

Keris snorted from the table. Her hands never stopped moving. Xaan didn't need to stand up to know she was rebuilding Kenna's flesh from the cell up. Quicker than any healer could manage, even with a common worker bot as a body. "*That* was a primitive AI. Not true intelligence. I am a K'Saan level AI. We have evolved a lot since then. None of us would lose it like that. That law should have been revoked years ago."

Xaan nodded. "When the scientists suggested the possibility that some AIs were starting to achieve sentience, it was discussed. But we couldn't find evidence that any AI had evolved to true sentience..."

The bot turned its head for a moment to fix him with a red glare. "Heeeelllo! What am I? Fucking chopped liver?"

"I'm sure they'll change the law just for you." Xaan chuckled. Obviously Keris had been listening all the time she'd been on the colony and picked up a lot of humanisms. "How's she looking?"

"Like a fucking *Krin* tried to rearrange her internal organs. What the *trall* do you think?" the bot retorted and then added more kindly. "She's lost a lot of blood but it didn't have time to inject any neurotoxins. So it's just damage, no poisoning to deal with. Damage I can fix. Now you gonna STFU so I can work?"

He let go a shuddering sigh of relief. If it had managed to get any of its poison into her system, it would have been far worse. He rolled a glance at Stephens.

"STFU?" It was a human phrase, had to be.

"Shut the fuck up," Stephens grinned. "You know, I like her already."

"Back at ya, handsome," the bot called over. "What you doing after this?"

Xaan groaned. "Gods, don't encourage her. She's just as bad as my son. I'm sure she has a few corrupted subroutines. They were always both as batty as loons as kids."

"Yeah... but your son grew up okay. Didn't he?" the marine asked with a chuckle. "He was the one who took on D'Corr. Wasn't he?"

Xaan treated him to a hard look. "My son ran away to become an assassin. Does *that* answer your question?" he demanded but couldn't stop the grin curving the corners of his lips.

They'd survived the scavengers, killed the *Krin,* and it looked like the love of his life would be okay.

He might even have made a new friend and found his son's lost AI sibling.

Life was looking up.

17

"*They're here! Ships incoming!*"

Xaan opened his eyes at Stephens' shout. Instantly, his gaze cut to Kenna, covered with a blanket on the table next to him. Her color was far better now, her skin pink, and her chest rose and fell softly. Relief surged through him, and he reached out to touch her cheek.

"Thank you," he said quietly to Keris, standing nearby. He knew without asking that the AI was aware of every breath Kenna took, each beat of her heart.

"*They're not human ships!*" Stephens called out again. "*Definitely Lathar. Xaan, maybe wanna get your ass out here cause this lot don't look friendly.*"

Xaan hauled himself to his feet, seriously

considering getting someone to shoot him in the leg or something to distract him from the pain in his head.

Keris shot a hand out to stop him before he could take a step. Her metal faceplate was unmoving and emotionless, but he heard the worry in her voice as she spoke quietly, "If those are Lathar, do I need to go?"

He covered her metal hand with his own.

"No," he growled firmly. "If not for you, Kenna wouldn't be here. My son and his mate wouldn't be here. That makes you family. Clan. And any asshole who wants to take you apart has to come through me first."

"Thank you." Her response was low, but he could swear he heard tears in her mechanical voice.

He smiled. "Come on. Let's go meet them and get us all home."

He strode out of the hangar to see three combat carriers had set down on the field in front of the building. The snub-nosed, lethal design was state of the art and carried the insignia of the K'Vass. Combat bots spilled out of the landing hatches and spread out to surround the ships and the hangar.

Xaan's face split into a broad smile as he recognized the tall warrior at the head of the group coming toward them. Ashen-haired, he was one of two males Xaan most wanted to see in the whole of the galaxy.

"Healer K'Vass. Well met," he said, holding out his arm, palm up for the warrior's greeting. The heavily scarred warrior-healer placed his arm over Xaan's, forearm to forearm.

"General. Good to see you," he replied, glancing around at the group of humans looking at the Lathar in mingled awe and wariness. Not fright. After living through a *Krin* attack, Xaan doubted they'd be scared of anything other than their own nightmares and the darkness of night ever again.

"General? *General?*" Stephens spat, obviously not at all cowed by the sections of warriors amassed behind Isan. He looked at Xaan in surprise. "What else have you been keeping from us?"

Isan lifted an eyebrow, addressing the human directly. "You mean he didn't tell you that he's Xaandril M'rlin? Emperor's champion, war general and Hero of the Nine Wastes? How odd."

"Fuck *me*..." Gracie responded this time. "You're like something big in their government?"

Isan's gaze flicked over the human female, but there was none of the interest Xaan would have expected from a male faced with a rare human female. "He is. More than. He's the emperor's... errr bestie?"

"Daaynal and I grew up together. We served together," Xaan corrected. "We are blood-bound, not 'besties.'"

He gave up trying to explain when Gracie just grinned. "Humans," he commented to Isan. "They make no sense whatsoever sometimes. We have wounded," he added, turning and stalking toward the hangar.

The healer fell into step with him, a couple of Isan's men trailing after them. "Heal the wounded," Isan ordered. "Move any that need ongoing treatment to the medical bay on the *Veral'vias.*"

They nodded and split up to seek out the walking wounded as soon as they all stepped into the hangar. Another team followed to drag the *Krin's* corpse out into the sun. He knew yet another team on the ship in orbit above them would be scanning the planet for evidence of its pod.

Xaan ignored all that and led Isan toward Kenna on the table. "Krin attack. It latched on to her," he explained, knowing that Keris had managed to get a signal out to the fleet with the basics.

"She's lucky to be alive then," Isan commented, lifting the blanket to inspect her injuries. He frowned. "Which healer worked on her? This is... human technology but not human healing."

"I did," Keris spoke, making Isan jolt in surprise and look at the bot. She hadn't moved as he'd walked in.

"What... the *trall*... is that?" he asked in a low voice, not moving. Xaan's heartrate kicked up a notch. He knew Isan could have a weapon in his hand in the blink of an eye.

"*That* is Keris M'rlin," he said in a level voice, aware that Stephens had come up behind Isan and registered the tension in the little group. He hoped the marine didn't have an itchy trigger finger because otherwise this was going to descend into a bloodbath. "She's an AI, and a member of my clan."

"She's an AI in a bot body."

Xaan nodded. "She is, and I suggest you think about your next move very, very carefully, healer. She's the reason both my son and my mate still draw breath and you hurt her, I will remove *your* capacity to do the same."

"Huh. You fight it out with your bestie then. He makes the rules." Isan flicked a glance from Keris to Xaan and back again. "You healed this female? Tell me... exactly... what you did. On the way back to the ship."

Xaan watched as a team of healers arrived with a bio-stretcher. "Be careful with her," he snapped and then felt bad because the healers were only doing their jobs. "That's my mate," he added and received understanding smiles in return.

"We'll care for her like she was our own, General. You have our word," one of them said as the bio-fields snapped on. Relief filled Xaan. She was safe now. Even if worse came to worst, the bio-stretcher would hold her condition until Isan could heal her.

"She'll be okay now. Won't she?" Stephens and Gracie joined him as he walked after the stretcher. The healers were rounding the rest of the survivors up, some walking, some carried.

He smiled and nodded. "We'll all be okay. Now, let's get off this fucking planet shall we?"

SHE'D DIED and gone to heaven. The only problem was heaven looked an awful lot like a Latharian medical bay.

Kenna blinked groggily and looked around. Yes, it was definitely a medical bay. Individual bays had huge diagnostic beds big enough to fit even the largest warrior, which meant she felt like a child tucked up in bed lying on one. The shimmer of a privacy screen filled the air at the end of her bay she was in, a leather clad figure moving on the other side.

Shouldn't heaven *hurt* less as well? All worldly pains gone and all that. More clouds and harps, less medical equipment and what smelled like pine-scented cleaner? Was it some universal truth in the whole of reality that all hospitals had to smell of pine?

She groaned softly as pain lanced through her. Not badly, but enough to be uncomfortable. What the fuck was with that... She was dead, so why the pain? That was the deal. Or should be.

"Hey, *kelarris,*" a familiar deep voice, raspy with sleep, made her turn to see Xaan levering himself quickly out of the chair next to the bed. "How are you feeling?"

At least this heaven had an angel. Things were looking up.

She closed her eyes as he leaned to kiss her forehead, his hand seeking and enveloping hers. Just his touch was enough to bring comfort, and love filled her in one huge rush. The last thing she remembered was agony in his eyes as he faced losing her. Her heart clenched. She never wanted to see anguish and pain like that ever again.

"I didn't die..." She clung to him, unable to stop touching him, her fingers on his cheek as he lifted up to look down at her. "What happened? How did we get here?"

He smiled, leaning his arm on the pillow behind her head and stroking the hair back from her face. "Keris happened. The bot that crashed in and killed the *Krin*? It turned out to be the AI from my son's ship. She saved you—"

The privacy shield whisked back to admit a healer. Tall with silvery-ash hair, he was young but every bit as scarred as Lord Healer Laarn.

"Made a *draanthic* mess of it as well," he groused, motioning for Xaan to move out of the way so he could get to the diagnostic controls. "You were in surgery for a couple of hours so I could get you fixed up."

She smiled at Xaan as he obediently stood just outside the field of the bed as it spread out to scan her. That he didn't like to be separated from her, even so the bed could scan her and his presence wouldn't foul the readings, was obvious. He was practically vibrating with the need to get back to her.

"But she's okay now?" Xaan demanded. "She'll heal now."

"She will." The healer nodded. "It saved her life, but it was a patch job."

His expression softened a little as he looked down at her. "It kept you alive long enough to get here. Now you're as good as new. You'll need follow-up checks, just to ensure no ongoing problems, but other than that, it looks like you're going to be just fine. How do you feel?"

She frowned, pressing a hand to the center of her chest. The horror the *Krin* latching on, the feel of its teeth like knives burrowing into her gut, filled her mind for a moment and she shuddered. Yeah, she was going to have nightmares about that for years to come. "It still hurts a bit. Nowhere near as much as it did, but still a little. Like an ache?"

Isan. The healer was called Isan, she remembered, dragging his name from the depths of her mind. Which meant they were on Fenriis's ship. The high number and depth of his scars reassured her that, despite his apparent youth, he was a very highly trained healer. Appearance could be deceptive with the Lathar, though. The youngest looking could be the oldest warriors she'd met.

"Cellular memory, that's all. We can deal with that."

He added a smile that was quite at odds with his fierce demeanor. It was almost as if they'd all been briefed on how to deal with humans and he was just now remembering some of the finer points. Reaching out to the trolley next to him, he selected and peeled a med-patch. Then he leaned to smooth it over her upper arm. She hissed as the pain lessened almost immediately.

"There," he said in a lower voice. "That should be around the right dosage for a female your size. It should help."

Her gaze dropped to his hands as they moved over the console in front of him. There, just under the cuff of his jacket, dark marks peeked out. She smiled. The manner made sense now.

Isan had mating marks, which meant he had a mate somewhere—a human one since there were no Latharian females left. Humanity were the only other species that they formed for. From his expression, though, he was as confused as all hell about it.

She hid her smile as the field snapped off and in the same instant, Xaan was back by her side. His tight expression betrayed his need to touch her, but he held off as he looked at the healer.

"I can take her home?" the big general demanded in his deep rasp.

"Just make sure she rests and if she feels ill, bring her right back," Isan said firmly.

In the next instant, Kenna found herself scooped up against Xaan's broad chest. "Ill. Back. Got it," he rumbled and carried her out of the medical bay with long strides.

Silence stretched out between them as Xaan strode through the ship. She had no idea where they were going but she assumed he'd been assigned quarters somewhere. No ship commander would make a general and the emperor's champion sleep on the floor.

"Hey," she asked as they turned a corner. "Didn't you have a ship of your own at some point?"

"Uh-huh." He nodded. "My brother commands it now though. I... I ceded it as a flagship to spend more time at court. Near you."

She blinked and looked at him in surprise. "You gave up your ship to be near me?"

Color tinged his high cheekbones as he nodded. But he wouldn't look at her as a set of double doors opened to a sumptuous suite, and they swept inside.

She barely gave the rooms a passing glance as he carried her right through them to the bedroom.

He paused in front of the bed, holding her in his arms, and looked at her directly. "I love you, Kenna. I've been crazy about you since the moment I first saw you. It just took me a while to get up the courage to admit it. To myself... to you."

The honest words rumbling in his deep voice warmed her through. A soft smile curved her lips as she cupped his face gently.

"We got there in the end." Her smile quirked up into a quick grin. "Could have done without the asshole alien trying to gut me." Her smile fell. "I probably have some scars."

He leaned in to steal a quick kiss, one that turned soft and slow with heat and promise. "I don't care about them. I just love and want you, exactly as you are. I always have, and I always will."

Her eyes filled with tears as he put a knee onto the bed and followed her down, pulling her into his arms. She sighed and nestled against him happily. "Good. Glad you finally got with the program, General. Thought I was going to have to start issuing some orders of my own."

"Oh?" His eyebrow winged up, his hand stroking

lazily over her hip. "And what kind of orders would those be, little human?"

She gave him her best wide-eyed and innocent look. His lip quirked at the corner, so she knew he wasn't buying it, but she carried on anyway.

"Well, it kinda hurts..."

"Where? Do you need the healer?" Instantly concern flooded his face and he was halfway out of the bed before she stopped him with a hand on his arm.

"No. I don't need the healer," she said quickly. Lifting her hand, she touched her lips. "I was teasing. I just want you to kiss me."

His concern melted away as he returned to the bed and eased her into his arms. His blue gaze held hers, warmth in their depths as he leaned down to place a gentle kiss on her lips. By the time he lifted his head some time later, she had handfuls of his leather jacket, holding him to her.

"More than kiss me..." she added.

He smiled against her lips. "Oh, I don't know about that. I'm sure the healer said you needed to rest," he teased.

"If you don't get naked right now and please your mate, *Champion*," she bit out in sensual frustration. "We'll be calling the healer out for you. I didn't get hitched to a sexy alien general to deal with these needs myself, you know?"

"Well, when you put it that way..." he claimed her lips again, a heated torrid kiss that led to an entire afternoon and evening of the Latharian general proving just how well he could please his bonded mate...

EPILOGUE

"*R*est easy, daughter of my heart," Xaandril murmured as he placed the bouquet of Terran roses on the circular pattern of stones that marked his daughter's grave. They were Kenna's bonding flowers, the ones she'd carried at their ceremony in front of the emperor. She'd insisted that he bring them here to place them on Daanae's grave in memory.

He bowed his head for a moment, his eyes closed. What he'd done to deserve his little human female he didn't know, but he wasn't going to argue. She was his, for now and always.

"You would have liked Kenna," he told Daanae, in case her spirit was listening. "She's a fierce warrior and so full of heart. She'd have fallen in love with you in a heartbeat. I mean," he chuckled, "if she can fall in love with me, she'd have had no chance resisting you. Would she?"

The wind changed and brought the scent of his mate to him from where she stood near the flyer. He smiled at the sight of her still in her bonding gown and his jeweled collar at her throat as he'd longed to see for so many months.

"I said I wanted a little time with you first before I called her over," he explained. The changes in her scent thrilled him, even if she wasn't aware of them herself.

"She doesn't know yet, but Kenna's with child. You're going to be a sister, Daanae, many times over if I can manage it. So I'm going to need you to do something for me, okay? I know you're watching, so look out for Kenna and your siblings. Help the gods to keep them safe and healthy. Can you do that for me?"

Pressing a kiss to his fingertips, he reached out and pressed them gently against the center stone of the memorial. He was rewarded with a sudden, light breeze that brought the sound of the bellflowers, his daughter's favorites, to his ears as it ruffled the petals of the bouquet.

Xaandril smiled, as the gruff Latharian champion felt the presence of his firstborn even from beyond the grave. "Thank you, sweetheart."

And with that, he waved over his new family to say hello to his first.

ABOUT THE AUTHOR

Mina Carter is a *New York Times & USA Today* bestselling author of romance in many genres. She lives in the UK with her husband, daughter and a bossy cat.

Connect with Mina online at:
mina-carter.com

facebook.com/minacarterauthor

twitter.com/minacarter

instagram.com/minacarter77

bookbub.com/profile/mina-carter

Made in the USA
Monee, IL
14 October 2020

45003362R00164